A Flair for Shamrocks

A Flair for Shamrocks

A Sadie Kramer Flair Mystery

Deborah Garner

CRANBERRY COVE PRESS

For all who love mystery, chocolate, and shamrocks
– or any combination of the above.

The Paige MacKenzie Mystery Series

Above the Bridge

The Moonglow Café

Three Silver Doves

Hutchins Creek Cache

Crazy Fox Ranch

Sweet Sierra Gulch

The Moonglow Christmas Series

Mistletoe at Moonglow

Silver Bells at Moonglow

Gingerbread at Moonglow

Nutcracker Sweets at Moonglow

Snowfall at Moonglow

Yuletide at Moonglow

Starlight at Moonglow

Joy at Moonglow

The Sadie Kramer Flair Series

A Flair for Chardonnay

A Flair for Drama

A Flair for Beignets

A Flair for Truffles

A Flair for Flip-Flops

A Flair for Goblins

A Flair for Shamrocks

Other titles:

Cranberry Bluff

Sweet Treats

ONE

Stuck on the side of the road wasn't where Sadie Kramer had intended to be on a cold, breezy, overcast day in the middle of March. Yet that was exactly where she found herself, alone except for Coco, her sidekick and companion Yorkie, who accompanied her everywhere.

It had seemed like a great idea, taking a road trip up the coast, out of California, along the coastline of Oregon, ending up in Portland. It was a city with much to offer, from the exquisite Japanese Gardens to Powell's, a fabulous bookstore with tons of selection. Sadie had recently taken to reading more—voraciously one might say. Mysteries, in particular, satisfied her desire for adventure. There hadn't been much of that lately in her life. It had been a slow few months of working at Flair. She adored her shop, which offered a variety of unique clothing and accessories. She never tired of fashion, being one to dress on the wild side herself. Neither did she tire of having a boutique next door to a gourmet chocolate shop. Her addiction to chocolate was well known. That was just one perk of going in each day, being able to hop next door for a fix whenever she wanted. The owner, Matteo, also had a habit of bringing samples over, which was welcome.

Still, there were days she didn't need to go in, thanks to

Amber, her ace assistant. And those days, sitting in a comfortable wing-backed chair in front of the picture window in her San Francisco penthouse—courtesy of her late husband, a real estate developer—she'd taken to reading, Coco curled up by her side in her own miniature wing-backed chair, custom upholstered in a floral print to match her own. There she devoured the likes of Agatha Christie, P. D. James, and Sir Arthur Conan Doyle.

Of course, she had a habit of falling into mysteries herself, often when traveling. Perhaps that had been her intention when she set off on the road. If not in search of a mystery, then simply for the adventure of not knowing what lay ahead, which was part of the mystery of life. In the end, in Portland, she'd end up in a store that could—and would—provide her with tote bags of new mysteries to solve, all packed into sweet-smelling pages and between fascinating covers that taunted her to see what they held inside.

However, being stranded on the side of a coastal highway was not the mystery she had anticipated when she'd left San Francisco behind and headed out on the road. This left her in a predicament, an unexpected one at that.

She pulled out her phone, dismayed to find herself in an area of the coast without service. Stepping out of the car to see if that might help her connect, she found it to be the same. This presented a conundrum. Should she start walking, Coco along with her, of course, in the tote bag she was used to riding in? Was she close to a town, or would she be walking for miles with no result other than sore feet from the impractical leopard-print flats she'd worn that day? Perhaps she should wait to see if some kind stranger pulled over to help. Again, a conundrum. How was she to know a kind stranger from a dangerous one these days? Visions of scenes from the recent books she'd read popped into her head, none of them appealing. For a brief moment, she wondered if she might be better off reading sweet romance books instead.

Leaning against the car, she felt a raindrop hit her forehead, then another on her forearm. Just what she needed. She sighed, got back in the car, and ran a hand over Coco's head while debating what to do.

A good fifteen minutes passed, maybe twenty, maybe thirty. Finally the sound of tires on gravel caught her attention, and she looked up to find a car pulling up behind her. She rolled her window down but kept the door locked as a man got out of the car and approached.

"Are you all right?"

It did seem a reasonable question, considering her situation. She'd turned on her flashing lights in hopes a police car or tow truck might happen by. The man seemed harmless, a fellow she guessed to be in his late thirties. He had a kind face and took a casual stance at a respectable distance from her door. She rolled her window down a little more.

"I seem to be having car trouble," Sadie said.

"What kind of trouble?"

That struck Sadie as a silly question, though she knew the man meant well. If she knew what kind of problem it was, she wouldn't be sitting on the side of the road. Then again, she might.

"I'm not sure. The car was running fine. I pulled over to let Coco out"—she glanced at the petite canine and then back at the man—"and when I tried to start the car again, it wouldn't start."

"I see," the man said. "Mind if I take a look under the hood? Can you pop it open?"

Sadie did as asked. The man looked under the hood and then returned to her window, leaving the hood propped up.

"I can't tell anything here. Could be several things. You're going to need to take it into town."

"Are you a mechanic?" This could be a stroke of luck.

"No, but there's a good one in town. I can give you a ride there, about ten miles up the road."

"Thank you, but I'd prefer to wait right here." There was no way Sadie was getting in a vehicle with a stranger. To ward off any forward moves, she added, "I have my guard dog with me." She pointed to Coco, and the man struggled to hold back a laugh.

"Have it your way," the man said. "I'll stop there and have them send a tow truck. My name's Finnian, by the way. Finnian Sweeney."

Sadie suddenly regretted her decision to leave home at all. There was plenty of adventure to be had without even stepping outside her door. She could have been eating raspberry truffles and reading a Louise Penny novel or getting lost in an Inspector Gamache story instead of the one she was in. Still, a tow truck was a better alternative to sitting on the side of the road. She'd have to accept the offer.

"Fine. I'd appreciate that."

"You're sure I can't give you a ride?"

"I'd rather just wait," she said, hoping she sounded more polite than paranoid. She pulled a copy of *Murder on the Orient Express* out of her open tote bag on the passenger floor and waved it nonchalantly. "I have a good book with me."

"Ah," Finnian said as if they were old friends. "I've read that one. The guilty party may not be who you think."

Sadie found that amusing. "It's my third time reading it, so I imagine it will be. It never seems to change." She mentally patted herself on the back, snark being one of her keener traits. Coco, quiet so far, yipped to back her up.

"I suspect you're right," Finnian said. "A tow truck should be here within an hour, I imagine."

"Thank you," Sadie said. "I appreciate your help." She opened her book and smiled at Mr. Sweeney's back as he slid into his car and continued along the road.

Two

Ayip from Coco caused Sadie to look up from her book. A southbound tow truck was making a U-turn on the highway just across from her car. As she expected, it pulled up in front of her, and a man stepped out. He was tall and slender, looking indeed mechanic-ish in overalls and a T-shirt. He wore a baseball cap turned backward and work boots that meant serious business.

Feeling slightly more assured than she had when Finnian had stopped, Sadie exited her car and greeted the approaching man.

"Thank you for coming out here," Sadie said. She noted the name Grady embroidered on his overalls.

"Not a problem," Grady said. "Finnian stopped by the shop and told me you were stranded. We couldn't just leave you here, could we?"

Knowing that was a rhetorical question, Sadie almost didn't answer. But for the sake of conversation, she spoke. "I appreciate that. There's no cell reception, so I couldn't call anyone."

Grady nodded. "Yep, that's the case out here most of the time. One day we might have reception, the next day we don't. Many of us have a landline for that reason, though I hear that's a dying species."

"Apparently," Sadie said. When was the last time she had a landline at home? Ten years? Fifteen? She had one at Flair, but that wasn't unusual for a shop.

Grady looked the car up and down, admiring it. "Sure is a pretty one. You're not looking to sell it, are you by chance?"

Sadie smiled. That wasn't the first time she'd heard the request. She'd had offers shouted to her at stoplights. But the possibility she'd let go of the bright red 1965 Mustang she drove was nonexistent. "Sorry, not a chance. I love this car. It belonged to my late husband."

"I understand. I wouldn't let it go myself. Never hurts to ask though. So let's see what's going on here." Grady walked around to the front of the car and looked under the hood. After playing around with a few wires and knobs, he attempted to start the car to no avail. He gave it a second try with the same results. "Yep, we're going to need to take this into the shop. Can't get it started. It could be the battery, but I won't know until I look at it more closely." He closed the hood gently, a move that Sadie appreciated. "Let's hook you up and take this baby to town."

"I need to get Coco." She reached into the vehicle, grabbing her tote bag with one hand and Coco with the other. She turned back to find Grady smiling.

"I take it this is your guard dog," Grady said. "Finnian told me to be careful. No wonder he was laughing when he said it."

Coco straightened up in Sadie's arms and let out a loud yip.

"She likes to be taken seriously," Sadie said by way of an explanation. She placed Coco gently in the tote bag, after which the Yorkie's head immediately popped back out and added another yip to the discussion. "Very seriously."

"Duly noted," Grady said. "Why don't we get the two of you in the tow truck. I'll hook up the car, and we'll head to town."

"I hope it's not anything important," Sadie said. "We're on our way to Portland, planning to get in tonight."

"Make that *hoping* to get in tonight," Grady said. "Let's see what's up with your car first. These classic cars sometimes require special parts that have to be ordered in."

That was a dismaying thought, but Sadie told herself not to worry yet. No news was still optimistic news as far as she was concerned. The coastal town was bound to be charming. She could wander around, maybe do some shopping, and when they called to say the car was fixed, she'd pick it up and continue to Portland. Yes, that was the plan. It would be fine.

Grady managed to hook up the Mustang without delay. Sadie climbed into the front seat of the tow truck, cradling the tote bag with Coco in her lap. The drive was short but pleasant with views of the ocean beyond beach grass and sand dunes. It reminded her why she'd taken the coastal route as opposed to simply heading up Interstate 5. Destination was important but so was the journey.

They pulled into what Sadie assumed to be the outskirts of a town after about fifteen minutes on the road. Conveniently, the garage was located in a gas station just past a sign that said Irishton. The building was weathered from surf and sand blowing against its painted walls over the years. It housed one service bay and a small convenience store where motorists could purchase snacks and beverages while filling up their cars. Sadie attempted to sit in a waiting area just off the service area but soon felt restless. Looking for options, she waited until Grady passed through and then asked him for suggestions.

"Grady," she said, hoisting her tote bag over her shoulder. "It looks like the rain has let up. How far is it to town? Could I walk there?"

Grady looked half-confused and half-amused. "Walk where?"

"You know," Sadie said. "Wherever there are shops I could browse while waiting for the car to be repaired. I could do a little shopping to pass the time."

"I hate to be the one to tell you this," Grady said. "But this is the town."

"This is a gas station."

Grady nodded and then took her elbow and escorted her to

the front window. He pointed across the street. "And a market and a pub and a post office. There are some residences beyond those buildings."

"I don't see a post office," Sadie said.

"It's inside the market." Grady looked at Sadie as if that were the most natural thing in the world.

"That's it?"

"That's it," Grady said. "What you see is what you get."

Sadie sighed. That was not at all what she'd pictured when her car was being towed from the side of the road. Where were the cute shops selling art and T-shirts and seashell sculptures and tacky jewelry? Where were the little cafés that specialized in chowder and other seafood delights? The residents with interesting stories to tell? The local newspaper, filled with unusual gossip not seen in major papers? Where was the *town*?

"No shops?" Sadie said, her tone touching on desperation.

"The market sells a few trinkets."

"A bookstore?"

"There's a shelf at the market..."

"A T-shirt stand?"

"The market..." Grady let his sentence wander off, the answer being obvious enough.

"Well!" Sadie exclaimed. "This is like falling into the *Twilight Zone*!" Coco followed that with a huff of sorts, a sound that resembled a cough as it emerged from the tote bag. Sadie took pity on the pup and lifted her out, where she stared out the window with a look as dismayed as that on Sadie's face.

"You're welcome to wait here," Grady offered, gesturing to the sculpted plastic chair that Sadie had been sitting in.

"I suppose I have no choice," Sadie replied. "There doesn't seem to be any place to go."

Grady rubbed his chin. "That's not necessarily true. You could head over to Quinn's place."

"Who is Quinn?" Sadie eyed Grady cautiously.

"Quinn Collins," Grady answered. "He owns the pub.

Decent guy, been running the pub for decades. It's the hot spot in this area."

Sadie felt skeptical about anywhere in the area being a hot spot and probably looked so, in view of Grady's next comment.

"It's just a suggestion. Something to do while you wait. Or feel free to stay here and enjoy our less-than-stellar coffee. Up to you." He pointed to a coffee maker on a short stack of shelves and returned to the garage.

Sadie debated the options. Gas station coffee didn't seem especially appealing. Neither did the idea of sitting and listening to the work going on in the service bay. Seeing the pub suggestion as possibly the best choice of those presented, she and Coco headed across the street to see what Quinn's place was all about.

THREE

The pub referred to as Quinn's place, though called O'PADDY'S according to a weathered sign hanging outside the front door, looked ramshackle at best from the outside. Inside, however, was a different story. It was well lit, boasting an impressive bar that Sadie guessed to be cherrywood, much like one she'd seen at the Irma Hotel in Cody, Wyoming, though not as big. That had been quite a sight, a gift from Queen Victoria to Buffalo Bill. This paled by comparison and surely didn't have royal history behind it, but it was still impressive, especially for a tiny coastal pub in a roadside hamlet that barely passed as a town.

To one side of the cozy interior, several small tables with laminate tops filled a third of the space. Across from those, a pool table took up the larger part of the area. A dartboard hung beyond that, dangerously close to the pool table in Sadie's opinion. It wouldn't take much for a wayward dart to ruin someone's mood. She hoped the establishment stocked a good first aid kit behind the bar.

Not seeing anyone either in the common areas or behind the bar, Sadie wandered along the walls, taking in maps of Ireland, photographs of Irish villages, and landscape paintings that resembled images she'd long had in her head when it came to that country. She'd never been there, though she'd traveled a fair amount back when her third husband Morris was still alive. But Ireland had always been on her bucket list. Perhaps this town could fill that desire today.

Then again, maybe not. This wasn't Ireland, and it wasn't Portland where she thought she'd be by this time. As roadside delays went, she supposed it could be worse. After all, she'd been rescued quickly, if the ride from Grady could be considered a rescue. And at least there was a pub here, which meant she could grab something to eat while waiting for her car. Yes, it could be worse.

Sadie looked at a shamrock-shaped clock on the wall, noting the time. How long could a minor car repair take? An hour? Two? She'd be on her way to Portland soon, the small town of—what was its name anyway, the place where she'd broken down? Oh, Irishton—just a memory of a stop along the way, an inconvenience, one of those things that came with a road trip.

The sound of shuffling feet drew her attention back to the bar, where she spotted a young man in his thirties—such was her guess—carrying a carton with a beer company logo on the side. He set it on the back bar counter, opened a cabinet, and flipped a couple of switches. A lilting Celtic tune began to float through the room. Turning toward the front, he then noticed Sadie.

"Greetings!" His cheerful voice struck her as delightful as did his overall demeanor. What was it about the way people carried themselves that conveyed them as either friendly or off-putting before so much as a full sentence of conversation took place? With this young man—after all, anyone under forty looked young from her senior viewpoint—it was probably the relaxed manner of his stance, the calm smile, and maybe just an air of openness that couldn't be defined.

"Welcome to O'Paddy's. Can I get you something to drink?"

Sadie approached the counter, thinking a modest drink of the nonalcoholic sort—after all, she'd soon be back on the road—sounded refreshing.

"That sounds great… Rafferty," she said, noting his name tag. "How about some cranberry juice and soda? Maybe with a lemon twist if you have it."

"You can call me Raff. Everyone else does. It's more expedient." He poured a glass three-quarters full with cranberry juice, used the bar nozzle to add soda water, and ran a lemon twist along the rim of the glass. "Here you go." He set the drink in front of Sadie, sliding a green cocktail napkin underneath. "Just passing through?"

Sadie nodded as she took a sip of the drink. Her eyes opened wide as the carbonation reached her nose. "Yes, just briefly. My car had some trouble down the road. It's across the street now."

"So, are you checking in?" Raff began pulling bottles out of the carton, lining them up on the counter.

"Checking in?" The question struck Sadie as curious. What would she be checking into? Perhaps he meant checking out, as in checking out the town.

"Yes," Raff said. "To a room upstairs. Lodging." He gestured to a staircase to one side of the bar.

"Oh, no," Sadie said, now understanding. "I'm on my way to Portland. So you're a pub and a motel? Just like the market is a post office?"

"I wouldn't call it a motel," Raff replied with a look of mock disapproval. "We like to think of it as a bed-and-beer. Like a bed-and-breakfast but more entertaining."

"Bed and beer," Sadie said. "Well, that does sound original. Intriguing even. Maybe another time."

"Or maybe this time," a voice said.

Sadie turned to see Grady standing behind her. She hadn't heard him enter over the lively music. The expression on his face was less than encouraging. She had a feeling she knew where this was going.

"What do you mean, maybe this time?" She braced herself for the answer, which she somehow already anticipated.

Grady nodded to Raff. "You have a room for this lovely lady? She's not going anywhere until I get that gorgeous car of hers running." He gave Sadie a sympathetic look. "I'm sorry, but I'm going to have to order a starter solenoid. It'll take a couple of days to bring in, seeing as we've got a holiday coming up."

A holiday? It took Sadie a few seconds to connect the fact that Saint Patrick's Day was only two days away. Leave it to her to get stranded in an Irish pub for the occasion.

"Surely there must be a way to get the part quickly. This afternoon even?"

Grady shook his head. "Not a chance I can get it today. I can try for tomorrow, but it's not likely. Deliveries take an extra day or so to come out here to the coast, at least this remote section. You're probably looking at three days."

"Well!" Sadie sat back down and took a generous gulp of her drink, thinking it wasn't nearly strong enough for the circumstances. She looked at Raff, who reached under the counter and pulled out a metal hoop with several keys attached. He shook the keys in the air.

"Seriously?" Sadie sighed. "There's no other option? A Hilton? A Marriott? Maybe a Club Med?"

Raff jingled the keys again. "Your options are room two, room three, or room four."

"You don't have a room one?" Sadie weighed the numbers, thinking the first room might make for the easiest escape.

"Nope," Raff said. "Quinn uses room one for an office. He owns the place, and it's hard to get work done here in the pub. He does all the paperwork upstairs."

Sadie was almost certain she heard Raff mumble "supposedly" at the end of his sentence, but she couldn't be sure and decided not to push for clarification. If Raff had a conflict with the owner, it wasn't her problem.

"What do you think, Coco?" Sadie addressed her bag,

resulting in a raised eyebrow from Raff. A double yip emerged from the tote, to which Sadie answered, "I agree. Good choice." She turned her attention back to Raff. "We'll take room two please."

"We?" Raff eyed the tote curiously. "Dare I ask what you have in there?"

"Oh!" Sadie exclaimed. "Let me introduce you!" She reached into the bag, lifted Coco out, and held her up. Coco cuddled against Sadie's chest while keeping a keen eye on Raff, who took a miniature pretzel from a bowl of snacks and, after a nod of permission from Sadie, offered it to the Yorkie. Coco, never one to turn down a treat, eagerly accepted the pretzel and immediately began looking around for more.

"Maybe later, little one." Raff reached over and stroked Coco's head. Coco, in turn, gave his hand a lick of approval.

"You're best friends now," Sadie said as she placed Coco back in the tote. "I suppose I'd better go retrieve my bags from the car. Looks like I'm not going anywhere for now. What do I owe you for the drink?"

Raff waved her offer of payment away. "It's on the house. And here's the key to room two. It's located at the top of the stairs and down the hallway." He pulled a key off the key ring and handed it to Sadie. "We serve pub fare around dinnertime, so you don't have to worry about going hungry. And you get a free beer with your room, which I imagine you could use about now."

"Absolutely," Sadie said as she headed for the door. *Maybe even two.*

FOUR

Sadie picked her bags up at the car repair shop and returned to O'Paddy's by way of a ride from Grady, who insisted on not having her cross the coast highway on foot while lugging the large floral suitcase she'd packed for the trip. She might have packed lighter if she'd known she'd be carrying a suitcase around repair shops and pubs, but fashion was her mainstay, and she never traveled without a wide array of clothing and accessories.

Some of what she packed for trips was just a matter of familiarity and comfort, like having her pink flamingo pajamas with her. She simply couldn't head out on the road without them. The same thing applied to her shoe and accessory collection. Multiple choices always accompanied her. These were "must haves" in her book. Needless to say, she always left room for items she would pick up along the way. No road trip was complete without a little shopping thrown in.

Raff was in the process of taking drink orders from new arrivals at the bar, several men, middle-aged she guessed from their clothing and haircuts, though she couldn't see their faces. Rather than disturb Raff and the guests, Sadie decided to search out her accommodation on her own. She already had the key. With only four rooms, it was bound to be easy.

The stairway was narrow, as might be expected in an older building, reminding her of narrow mountain roads where one hoped a car wouldn't approach from the opposite direction. Two people passing on the pub's stairway would prove difficult, especially with a large suitcase and a Yorkie-toting bag along. Fortunately, she encountered no one on her way up the stairs, and she was soon standing in a dim hallway, illuminated only by two hanging light bulbs without shades of any sort.

Locating her room proved to be easy, as she expected, though she was surprised to find it at the very back of the building. The room numbers assigned to the doors ran in reverse order, with the third and fourth rooms closest to the front stairs and the first and second toward the back. This was a relief, considering it might place her farther away from late-night activity and noise if the pub became crowded. She didn't doubt that it would. There was nowhere else in the so-called town for anyone to go if they wanted to go out at night. It served as not only a local watering hole but also the only eatery around. *What sort of town doesn't have a pizza parlor?*

That thought reminded her to check out the pub menu in anticipation of dinner later. Maybe she wouldn't be able to order a combo pizza with extra cheese, but there'd be something she could have.

The door to her room creaked as it opened, and for a brief moment she had the urge to back away. Yet as she stepped inside, she was pleased, just as she had been when she first entered the pub, to find the room in good shape. It was neat, clean, and furnished with a mix of antiques and cozy additions: knit throws, fluffy pillows, a bookshelf with travel books on Ireland. Despite the dim hallway and creaking door, the accommodations were appealing and comfortable. She felt instantly better about staying upstairs over the pub, which had sounded less than ideal at first.

She closed the door and settled into the room, propping her

suitcase on a typical hotel luggage rack. She unzipped the bag and removed a few essential items: a toothbrush, toothpaste, a hairbrush, and some vitamins that she'd recently begun taking in a failing attempt to feel twenty years younger.

With those necessities arranged on an oak dresser, she then set up what she referred to as Coco's travel palace, an elaborate portable kennel lined with velvet and boasting a new set of china water and food bowls that she'd picked up recently at an estate sale. Coco, who had been so far cruising around the room, sniffing and examining the new surroundings, picked a comfortable spot in the fancy crate and curled up on a velvet pillow that complemented the overall lining of the structure.

"We seem to be on quite an adventure," Sadie said to Coco, who simply eyed her in return, her expression somewhat dubious, at least as dubious as a canine expression might be. "It's not the adventure we thought we were taking, but it's interesting nonetheless."

Coco sighed and put her head down, closing her eyes. Taking a cue from the dog's behavior, Sadie pulled out her copy of *Murder on the Orient Express* and stretched out on the bed, pleased to find it comfortable as well as home to an accumulation of fluffy pillows housed in pillowcases with an attractive plaid pattern that wasn't overly bright. After a mere five pages, the stress of the day caught up with her and she soon dozed off.

She awakened to find the light outside fading, a touch of sunset over the ocean showing through a paned window. The sound of faint music and voices reached her ears, and she suspected evening customers were starting to gather downstairs. She stood and stretched, then moved to the window where she saw several vehicles parked outside that hadn't been there earlier. She sighed. At least if she had to break down somewhere, she'd picked a popular place. With music, food, and a complimentary beer, it could have been worse.

"What do you say, Coco? Should we go check the action out?"

Coco lifted her head off the velvet pillow in response to Sadie's question and yawned, appearing at first uncertain and then willing. She stood, stretched, and exited the elegant kennel. Sadie fished a glittery green collar from her suitcase.

"I know we were saving this for Portland," Sadie said as she put the festive collar on the Yorkie. "But it seems appropriate to wear it here, all things considered. No harm blending in with the local culture."

Sadie considered changing into an outfit of her own that she'd brought in anticipation of wearing it in Portland for Saint Patrick's Day, but a rumbling sensation in her stomach made her reconsider. The outfit could wait. Food, it seemed, could not.

After helping Coco into her tote bag and gently draping the straps over her shoulder, she exited the room and locked the door. She turned in the direction of the hallway, which was when she stopped, eyes locked on an unexpected sight. Positioned in such a way as to block the stairway—whether intentionally or not—was a potbellied pig. That certainly wasn't something she'd expected to see in a lodging establishment or, for that matter, in a pub.

She took a step closer, thinking the creature might move out of the way or even run from her. But it didn't budge. Instead, it watched her intently, an action that Sadie returned in equal measure, which allowed her to further examine both the situation and the pig itself.

The unexpected porcine encounter was more surprising than scary. Sadie knew people sometimes had potbellied pigs as pets, and she'd heard they were quite intelligent. She'd just never come face-to-face with one before. As pigs went, this seemed to be a rather attractive specimen. It had a typical round snout, chubby cheeks, and the coloring of a spotted cow, which she determined after a sideways step that allowed her to view its portly body. It didn't strike her as overweight by pig standards, though she pondered the size of the body compared to the short, skinny legs and tiny hooves. To top it off, she could almost swear it was smiling at her. She'd known dogs to smile before, but a pig? Well, why not?

"Hello there," Sadie said, which turned out to be not the best move, as it caused Coco to climb the inside of her tote bag and peer over the top, immediately spotting the pig. Fortunately, it didn't result in a flurry of barking. Instead, Coco simply tilted her head to the side as if trying to decide what she was seeing. Sadie watched Coco with curiosity, and it occurred to her that she had no idea whether Coco had ever seen a pig before. She couldn't recall an occasion when they'd come across one.

Nudging Coco gently back inside the bag, Sadie took a few steps toward the pig, hoping this would encourage it to move aside. When that brought no result, she made the brave decision to walk past it. She eased herself around the pig to reach the top of the stairs. The pig, in turn, simply swiveled its head to watch her but held its place on the carpeted floor.

"Thank you," Sadie said, feeling only a tad bit silly for talking to a pig. It wasn't all that different from talking to Coco after all. If she could have a conversation with a dog, why not a pig?

Sadie made her way down the stairs, keeping one hand on the handrail and the other on her tote. She didn't want to take the chance of Coco jumping out to do a little pig research on her own. At the bottom of the stairs, she emerged into a cheerful scene of locals conversing over mugs of beer or shooting pool. Raff stood behind the bar, flirting with—or perhaps being flirted with by—two women in jeans and T-shirts with an O'Paddy's logo across the back. Sadie approached the bar and took a place beside them. Raff greeted her with a friendly smile, and she realized she felt somewhat like a local already.

"Raff..." She looked back, thinking perhaps she'd been followed downstairs. Seeing only the foot of the stairs, she turned back to the bartender. "There is a pig upstairs."

"Is there?" Raff said, a twinkle in his eye. "Are you sure?"

"Absolutely," Sadie insisted. "At the top of the stairs. You know, that potbellied kind. And it smiled at me! I'm not making this up." She threw another glance at the stairwell, but there was no sign of the culprit.

"Maybe you're ready for that beer," Raff suggested. "The one included with your room."

"Maybe you're right," Sadie said. "But that doesn't mean I'm making this up. There is a pig upstairs."

Raff poured a draft beer, set it in front of Sadie, and smiled. "I imagine you're talking about Paddy."

Sadie took a sip of her beer and leveled her eyes on Raff. "Paddy? The pig's name is Paddy? Paddy as in O'Paddy's?"

Raff nodded and then called over to a middle-aged man at the end of the bar. "Quinn, your pig's upstairs again."

The man rolled his eyes. "Thanks, Raff. I'll go get him. Hold my beer."

Raff turned back to Sadie. "Thanks for letting us know. Paddy has an adventurous spirit. He tends to wander."

"I didn't even know pigs could climb stairs." Sadie took another sip of beer, thinking this over. It had never occurred to her to wonder.

"They can, but it's not natural or easy for them." Raff nodded toward the man he'd called Quinn, who was heading for the stairs. "Paddy will climb up, but he's not thrilled about coming back down. Quinn's on his way to retrieve him."

"Well, he does seem like a friendly pig," Sadie said, suddenly wondering if she even knew what she was talking about. But the pig had smiled at her, right? Therefore, it stood to reason that it was a friendly pig.

With that thought, Sadie did the only thing that seemed reasonable. She chugged the rest of her beer and asked for another.

FIVE

With the mystery of Paddy solved, Sadie perused the menu. She was pleased to see the laminated sheet offered a good number of choices, including Irish stew, clam chowder, quiche, burgers, salads, and a variety of appetizers. Fried mozzarella sticks sounded appealing but so did loaded potato skins and sweet potato fries. She finally settled on an order of fish and chips, knowing that a chip or three could casually fall into her tote bag, thus keeping Coco content.

As the evening wore on, the pub filled and the noise level grew higher. Customers entered, some heading for the bar, others to the pool table, yet others through a nondescript door not far from the dartboard, which was where Quinn headed once he returned downstairs with Paddy. He emerged a few minutes later and reclaimed his seat at the bar. He took a couple of swigs of the drink he'd abandoned to go retrieve Paddy, announced that he was heading home, and left.

The crowd around the pool table consisted of mostly men, including one who looked especially rough. An attractive woman dressed to flaunt her curves also hovered near the table, feigning interest in the game but not well enough to be taken seriously.

Sadie suspected she might be looking to play something, but it likely wasn't pool.

Paddy, now reacquainted with the ground floor of the building, wandered around like any regular customer, appearing just as happy—though not nearly as tall—as any other guest. Amazingly, everyone seemed to know where he was from one moment to the next. No one tripped, no one squealed, and not a single crisis occurred that one might imagine happening with a pig loose in a pub.

"A pig in a pub, Coco," Sadie said as she dropped a fry, aka a chip, into the tote bag. "What do you think of that?"

"Does your purse ever answer you?"

Taken by surprise at the sound of a voice, Sadie turned to see Finnian beside her. He waved to Raff, who nodded and pulled a frosted mug from a refrigerated compartment. The unspoken beer order landed on the counter almost immediately.

"Good service here," Sadie said, noticing the routine that was surely repeated on a regular basis.

"The best," Finnian said. He raised his mug in a silent toast and took a hearty gulp. Setting the mug down on the counter, he eyed her tote bag. "You didn't answer my question. Does your purse ever answer you? Or perhaps you weren't really talking to it. I suspect you harbor that fierce guard dog of yours in there. Either that or your bag itself is hungry, a chilling thought, reminiscent of horror films. A carnivorous purse." He took another swig of his beer as if contemplating the idea.

"You need not fear either the bag or the dog," Sadie said. "They're both harmless. See for yourself." She opened the top of the tote and lifted Coco out. She then hesitated, looking around. "I suppose she shouldn't be out, being a food establishment and all."

Finnian laughed. "In case you haven't noticed yet, they're pretty lax about animals in here."

"Yes, I got that feeling. I met Paddy earlier," Sadie said. "Quite the surprise encounter. Seems like a... lovely... pig." Sadie chose her words carefully. What was the appropriate way to compliment a pig? Was there a standard she wasn't aware of? Some kind of pig etiquette she'd missed out on in school and social learning environments?

"Indeed, a lovely pig," another voice said.

Sadie turned to see Grady approaching, close enough to have overheard her comment. No longer in work overalls, he looked somehow younger in jeans and a blue-and-red flannel shirt. He gave Coco a pat on the head and then waved to Raff, who quickly poured a draft and set it on the counter in front of Grady. It was becoming clear to Sadie that locals could order by telepathy.

"Any more news about when the car part will come in?" Still hoping for the next day, Sadie was dismayed to see him shake his head.

Grady took a hearty gulp from his beer mug. "I'm afraid it'll be a couple of days. Sorry to not have better news for you."

"No way to rush it?" Sadie asked.

"I'm afraid not," Grady said. "I called the parts house again to see if they could get it here sooner, but they can't. Looks like you're in for an Irishton holiday. But look at the bright side: What better place to spend Saint Patrick's Day than in an Irish pub in a town called Irishton?"

Portland, Sadie thought. *Portland would be the better place.* She hugged Coco to her chest and sighed. It didn't seem she had a choice. Like it or not, Irishton was where she would be until her car could be repaired.

"Hey, Raff," Grady shouted as the bartender delivered a drink to a man a couple of seats away. "Is Quinn around? I need to talk to him."

"You just missed him," Raff called back. "He headed home. Want to leave him a message in case he comes back later?" He grabbed another frosted mug from the refrigerated compartment and began to fill a draft for a customer who'd just taken a seat at the counter.

Sadie noted the pub was filling up quickly now, some folks

arriving for drinks, some to join the growing crowd at the pool table, and some just to kill time and catch up on local gossip.

"Not necessary," Grady said. He took a couple more gulps of beer and stood. He patted the counter with one hand as a nonverbal sign of departure and then turned to Sadie. "Sorry about your car. Try to make the best of it. This can be a pretty interesting town." He headed for the door, tossing a "See ya, Raff. Put it on my tab" over his shoulder.

Sadie finished her drink and rummaged in her bag for money with one hand while holding Coco with the other. Coco, seemingly fascinated with the unfamiliar surroundings, placed both front paws on Sadie's shoulders, watching the activity.

"I suspect your beer is on the house," Finnian said. "They call this a bed-and-beer establishment."

"So I've been told," Sadie said. "But I had fish and chips as well. Oh, and I had a second beer. My goodness!" Having recited this for no reason at all, she suddenly felt like she'd confessed to a wild night on the town. That thought alone made her realize she was tired. It had been a long and quite unexpected day. She fished some bills out of her purse and placed them on the counter, enough to cover what she'd ordered plus a good tip. Saying good night to Finnian, she and Coco took a brief trip outside for Coco's benefit and then headed back to their room.

Six

Situated at the end of the hallway, Sadie would have expected the room to be somewhat quiet, but the noise from the pub floated upstairs. Rock tunes from the pub jukebox had replaced the calmer Celtic music that had been playing earlier in the day. Laughter echoed up the stairs and down the hallway as well as—to the best of Sadie's perception—through the heating vents. The one window in the room looked out over a parking lot on the side of the building, resulting in vehicle noise. She kept the window closed, but voices still drifted up as customers walked to their cars.

Sadie settled in for the evening with a book and a glass of water on a night table beside her bed. Coco escorted herself to her travel palace, curling up on the velvet and falling asleep almost immediately. Although Coco slept soundly, Sadie was unable to sleep. The events of the day, the unexpected landing in the quirky town, and the hum of continued pub activity kept her awake.

As time wore on, the noise downstairs decreased, eventually dwindling to merely low-volume music and clinking of bottles, which Sadie guessed to be from Raff cleaning up.

Just as it seemed sleep would come, a door outside slammed— not once but twice—and a heated argument began somewhere behind the building. The conversation itself was indecipherable, but there was no question the voices were angry. There were two, maybe three voices, all male. Sadie tried to differentiate the tones in hopes of determining how many were involved.

After five minutes or so, another even louder voice joined in, which she recognized as Raff telling the others to go home. The door slammed again, and the arguing turned to footsteps scuffling, engines starting, and vehicles leaving the parking lot.

The music stopped entirely a few minutes later, the back door sounded again, and another car left the lot. Peering out the side window, Sadie saw the lot was now empty.

Morning seemed to arrive almost immediately, and Sadie wondered if she'd even managed four hours of sleep. She tended to be an early riser, a habit that was not altered by the hour she went to bed. Early to bed, early to rise, or late to bed, early to rise were her only sleep cycles.

Dressed and ready for coffee long before the pub opened, she found her way outside via a staircase at the rear of the building since the interior entrance to the café was locked. Anxious to find her morning caffeine infusion, she walked to the market, which she was now tempted to call "the everything store." There she found not only the java fix she was seeking but also an enticing bakery counter and a decent opportunity to hear town gossip. As she poured cream into her take-out cup, she couldn't help but overhear a conversation an aisle away, one that shocked her awake before she even took a sip of coffee.

"I don't know what happened," a familiar—yet not quite identifiable—voice said. "I just know they found him at home this morning, dead as a doornail, as they say."

"It's hard to believe." A different voice.

"Not really. He probably had it coming." A third voice, relatively gruff and unsympathetic.

"That's a terrible thing to say!" Back to the first voice.

Indeed, Sadie thought to herself. *That is a horrible thing to say about anyone.* Which immediately brought her to the main question: Who were they talking about? Someone she'd already met? Someone else? She felt guilty as she found herself hoping they weren't talking about Paddy. But a pig couldn't "have it coming." This was definitely about a human.

She continued to listen in—some might call it eavesdropping—hoping to learn the identity of the victim, not that she'd met more than a handful of people. And then there were all the usual questions: Was this a result of foul play? Did the person simply pass away of natural causes or disease? Could there have been an accident of some sort?

"Must be about that back room. I bet he made someone angry."

Sadie's ears perked up at that. What about the back room? She remembered the door beside the dartboard and several people ducking in and out of there, the pub owner included. And there was the argument she'd heard outside, the one Rafferty broke up. Had a dispute come up in the back room that spilled outside? A disagreement between pub patrons? An altercation between the owner and someone else?

"Or something more personal," another voice said.

"I can't imagine anyone wanting to hurt Quinn."

This time Sadie was sure the voice was Grady's. She was struck with a whole new string of questions, starting off with her current accommodation. If the deceased was the pub owner, would the pub stay open? Would she be able to keep her room until her car was repaired? And what if she couldn't? Where would she go?

Sadie considered approaching the discussion, curious to confirm that Quinn was the victim. Instead, she chose to go to the cashier stand and pay for her coffee.

"Two dollars even," the woman behind the counter said.

Not a bad price, Sadie thought. It was certainly better than what she was used to paying in the city. She handed two crisp dollar bills across the counter, noting the woman's name tag said Susanna. It was a name Sadie had always been fond of, thanks to a sweet aunt who'd been a favorite of hers growing up. Based on that, she felt an immediate kinship with the woman as she handed the money over.

"Thank you," Susanna said as she put the bills in the register. "Are you just passing through town?"

"Trying to," Sadie said, keeping her voice low in hopes of staying out of the nearby conversation. Seeing a confused look on the woman's face, she explained. "Oh, I mean yes, I'm just passing through. My car broke down outside of town. It's over at the repair shop."

Susanna nodded. "Well, you'll be on your way in no time. Grady knows what he's doing. We all depend on him to keep our vehicles running."

"That's good to know. Thanks," Sadie said as she turned to leave. Had Coco not popped her head out of the tote and yipped, she might have made it out of the store unnoticed by anyone else. As it happened, the sharp yip drew attention, and Finnian emerged from the other aisle.

"Sadie! Good morning." Finnian's curly brown hair was partially covered by a beach-type hat, and he wore jeans, a red T-shirt, and a tan windbreaker. He looked surprised, perhaps even disappointed, to see her, which she attributed to the fact he assumed she'd overheard the conversation. Although there was nothing inappropriate about the discussion, it was hardly the type of news a local resident would want an out-of-town guest to wake up to. Sadie decided to not waste time tiptoeing around the issue.

"Finnian," Sadie said brightly. "Good morning! I couldn't help overhearing the conversation back there. It sounded like terrible news. I extend my sympathies." Coco yipped a few condolences of her own.

"Yes," Finnian said, clearly distressed. "It's horrible. The owner of O'Paddy's was found dead at his house this morning. Everyone's in shock."

Finnian looked over his shoulder at the sound of footsteps. Grady approached along with the rough-looking man Sadie recognized from the pool table the night before.

"Hello Grady," Sadie said. She looked at the other man, expecting an introduction of some kind. When none came forth, she introduced herself. Whether willingly or just feeling put on the spot, the man offered his name as Drew.

"Nice to meet you," Sadie said, knowing this was less than sincere. Nothing in the man's composure was appealing, and the wild thought that he might be behind whatever tragedy had befallen Quinn ran through her mind. *Do not judge a book by its cover*, she reminded herself.

"Drew owns a bar called Drew's Place a few miles up the road," Finnian offered.

"Far up the road?" Sadie asked, wondering if this might be competition for O'Paddy's.

"Not too far," Drew said. "About twenty miles."

"Not far enough," Grady mumbled at the same time.

Drew ignored Grady.

Whatever was going on between the three of them felt ready to escalate, not something Sadie cared to witness. Besides, it wasn't her business anyway. She ordinarily welcomed mysteries, but this place wasn't where she wanted to find one. She offered condolences again to the trio of guys and excused herself. The thought of spending a quiet morning in her room sounded appealing, and that was exactly what she planned to do.

SEVEN

Whatever peace Sadie expected to find back at the pub, her hope was quickly dashed. A police vehicle was parked at the foot of the back stairs. An officer stood beside it along with Rafferty, who looked pale and shaken.

Not knowing what else to do, Sadie approached. Where else was she going to go without transportation?

"May I help you?" The officer, a man of short stature, wearing a trench coat and hat that gave him a Columbo presence, addressed her formally as she walked up. "The pub is closed."

Coco, hearing an unexpected voice, peeked over the edge of Sadie's bag and eyed the man suspiciously. Rafferty, recognizing the situation, jumped in to explain.

"It's all right, Detective. She's a guest. She's staying here while her car is being repaired."

The detective clicked a pen and held it over a notepad. "Name? Place of residence? Destination? Purpose for your visit?"

Sadie, taken aback by the detective's interrogative style, sent Rafferty a questioning look. "Sadie Kramer. San Francisco. Portland. Car repair." She watched the detective scribble her answers down, noticing his name tag in the meantime.

"Detective Ross," Sadie said as he finished jotting down notes. "May I go on up to my room now?"

"The pub is closed. I'm afraid we can't let anyone inside until we inspect it."

Rafferty chimed in, much to Sadie's relief. "She's not entering the pub, Detective. She's only going to the lodging upstairs. That section is closed off from the main floor. She won't be able to enter the pub itself."

Sadie waited while the detective appeared to debate this, meanwhile wondering where she would go if not allowed in. There was nowhere else. Only the market and gas station. Neither seemed an ideal place to spend the morning.

On the other hand, perhaps being kept outside could be advantageous. Her curiosity was already kicking in about the sudden demise of the pub owner. She'd been helpful—much to the initial dismay of other detectives—on other occasions when she'd fallen into similar situations. The fact she *did* fall into them was curious, but it seemed to happen often, oddly enough. There was the time at the beach... the time at the winery... the time in New Orleans... Oh, what did it matter? She wasn't responsible for those unfortunate events. She just had an uncanny knack for being in the wrong place at the wrong time.

"Detective Ross," Sadie began. "Do you have any suspects?" The look she received in return made her certain she'd soon be able to go up to her room. Or maybe "sent to her room" was a better description.

"No one has determined any foul play, Miss... what is your name again?" The detective poised his pen above the notepad, reading his previous notes, which struck Sadie as not being a particularly good sign.

"Sadie Kramer. I'm passing through on my way to Portland."

"Portland." Detective Ross nodded as he jotted that down, his serious demeanor a tad excessive in Sadie's opinion.

"Yes," Sadie replied. "Portland. I had planned to spend Saint Patrick's Day there, see some sights, visit a favorite bookstore."

"Yet you ended up here."

Sadie sighed. "That was my car's decision, not mine. Like I said, I'm here to have it repaired. I wouldn't have chosen to stop in this town otherwise. If you can even call it a town." She turned to Rafferty. "No offense."

"None taken," Rafferty said.

"But you *are* here," the detective pointed out. "Just when the owner of the establishment you're staying at ends up dead." He turned to Rafferty. "Are there any other overnight guests?" He jabbed his pen in the air, pointing in the direction of the guest rooms.

Rafferty shook his head. "No one else. Sadie is our only guest."

"I see." Again the detective scribbled notes, which Sadie found not only unnecessary but disturbing. It was sheer coincidence that she happened to be there at all, much less alone.

"We don't usually rent rooms around this holiday," Rafferty explained. "In case we have customers who celebrate to excess and shouldn't drive. We had no choice with Sadie since her car broke down."

Well! Sadie thought. *That was hardly welcoming.* Yet it was true. They really didn't have any choice even if they intended to keep all the rooms open for cases of excessive imbibing, a worthy policy.

"No offense," Rafferty said, realizing the way his statement had come out.

"None taken," Sadie said. They were even now, each having unintentionally offended the other.

"It seems you're not involved," Detective Ross said, clicking his pen again. "You may go to your room."

Exactly the phrasing Sadie disliked. Suddenly she felt like a child being reprimanded. It had happened more than once in her younger years, often a result of either her curiosity or tendency to be outspoken. Then again, there was her disdain for creamed peas, which resulted in temporary isolation when she was around the age of nine. Or was it eight? So many decades ago.

"Or I could help you," Sadie countered. "I've helped detectives before."

"I'm sure they appreciated that," Detective Ross said, his tone remarkably sarcastic.

"Sometimes an outside viewpoint can be helpful," Sadie said.

Another pen click. "We'll be just fine, Ms. Kramer."

"Okay then!" Sadie started up the stairs, talking as she climbed the steps. "If you decide you'd like to hear about the fight outside last night, you'll know where to find me." As she reached the top landing and put her hand on the door handle, the response she expected came from below.

"What fight?"

Sadie turned back to face the detective and Raff, who had an unreadable look on his face. This reminded Sadie that one of the voices she'd heard had sounded like Raff telling those arguing to go home. But then... why wouldn't Raff be telling the detective about the argument already?

"I don't know much," Sadie said. "Only that there was a heated discussion out here last night. It sounded like two, maybe three people. I didn't recognize the voices. They all sounded like men."

"What time was this?" Detective Ross readied his pen again.

Sadie thought it over. She'd fallen asleep and hadn't checked the time when she heard the disagreement. But the pub noise had tapered off, so it stood to reason that it was late, around closing time.

"I'm not sure, Detective. I was trying to sleep. Maybe closing time? Around midnight? One o'clock? Somewhere in there?" Sadie glanced at Raff, wondering why he wasn't jumping in. She was certain he was the one who'd told the others to leave. He would know what time it was. Yet he said nothing. She caught his eye but couldn't read what was behind it.

"And you didn't recognize the voices at all?"

Now Sadie was getting frustrated. "I don't know anyone here, Detective. I only arrived yesterday. I've met a handful of people and one delightful pig. I had dinner and went to bed. That's my entire history here."

"No other observations?"

"The fish and chips are delicious."

"Anything else?"

"Only that there's no decent shopping here. The town really should open a few boutiques, maybe a nail salon. And a day spa too. Definitely a day spa." She was certain she saw Raff holding back a grin. Maybe the day spa comment had been a little much.

Detective Ross folded his notebook and slipped it into a front shirt pocket along with the pen. "Thank you. That will be all for now. If I have any more questions, I know where to find you."

Feeling sufficiently dismissed, Sadie nodded and continued inside the building. Once in her room, she sat on the bed, Coco beside her. Something odd was going on. For one thing, she had a hunch Raff knew more than he was letting on. Why hadn't he been more forthcoming about the late-night argument? Unless he wasn't the person who'd told the others to leave. But if not Raff, then who was it? She was sure the voice had been familiar. She tried to recall the voices of others she'd met there: Grady, Finnian... Could one—or both—of them have been involved? Or could Quinn have been part of that disagreement? She'd only heard his voice briefly that evening and wouldn't have recognized it.

She lifted Coco into her lap and ran her hand over the Yorkie's soft fur. There wasn't enough to go on. Which meant only one thing: she'd need to find out more.

EIGHT

Sadie checked the time and determined that it was late enough in the morning to call Flair. Her fashion boutique wouldn't be open for another fifteen minutes, but she knew her assistant, Amber, would already be there. She'd been fortunate to have the same assistant for years, starting off as a cashier, then promoted to assistant manager, and now fully in charge of handling all aspects of the store, which allowed Sadie more freedom for travel and personal time.

Amber could be counted on to show up early, even earlier than necessary. Her habit was to arrive well before the shop opened, caffeine-infused from stopping at Jay's Java Joint on the way. That was why Flair was always in perfect order when the doors opened each morning. Clothes hung neatly on racks, accessories waited in full displays, and the front window was attractive and tidy. The shop looked exactly like a boutique should look, one that beckoned shoppers to linger and get creative with their choices.

Amber answered the shop phone on the second ring, which surprised Sadie only because she'd half expected the dependable employee to be in the front display window, something she adjusted every morning, whether to change a sweater for variety or just to make sure everything was in order.

"Good morning!" Sadie said. "You must be at the counter to answer so quickly. I figured you'd be in the front window."

Amber laughed. "You know my habits too well. No, I already finished the front window. I put a leprechaun hat on Trudy and added a bright green cashmere sweater to her outfit. She looks especially festive."

The reference to Trudy caused Sadie to chuckle. They'd named the mannequin after a customer told them it resembled a cousin by that name. From that day forward, they'd referred to it as Trudy, which delighted them as it made dressing her seem more personal. Choosing outfits for Trudy had now become one of their favorite pastimes, and holidays offered a chance to be even more creative.

"I'm sure she looks wonderful," Sadie said. "Clever idea to give her a hat. In fact, I could use one myself about now."

"I imagine you could find one if you looked around. Maybe even a matching one for Coco. How's Portland?"

"About that..." Sadie stopped midsentence, interrupted by a firm knock on the door. She told Amber to hold on while she answered it, phone still to her ear. Somehow she was not surprised to find Detective Ross on the other side.

"Detective," she said, attempting a welcoming smile that was anything but that. As she lowered the phone, she was certain she heard Amber say, "Not again." This was the reaction she'd expected. She'd just hoped to explain the situation herself, in private, where she could at least embellish it a tad.

"Ms. Kramer," the detective responded. "I have a few more questions for you. Would you mind coming outside?"

"Not at all," she said. "Let me finish this call. I'll meet you in just a few minutes."

"I'll be downstairs. *Waiting.*" The last word was clearly a request, more likely a command, for her to end the phone call quickly.

Sadie closed the door and lifted the phone back to her ear. She wanted to give Amber an explanation, however brief. She opened her mouth to speak, but Amber beat her to it.

"How on earth do you end up in these situations?"

"I have no idea. It seems someone dies every time I go on vacation. Maybe I should never leave the house."

"That's an idea," Amber said. "Then again, people die every day, probably every minute. Staying home wouldn't prevent that."

"Good point," Sadie said. "I just wish they wouldn't do it wherever I go when I take trips. It's unsettling. I seem to be collecting detectives when I travel instead of souvenirs."

"Speaking of detectives, I've been meaning to ask..."

Sadie knew where Amber was going. There was one detective in particular that she'd "collected" who had remained a part of her life. Detective Broussard had helped solve a case in New Orleans, and the two had formed a strong bond that was a mixture of friendship and romance. The long-distance relationship had kept it from growing more serious, but the potential was there. The thought made Sadie smile, but she quickly snapped back to the situation at hand.

"We can catch up on that later," Sadie said. "Right now I'm needed downstairs for some reason."

"That reason being the demise of someone there in Portland?"

Sadie started to explain her predicament but opted to wait, knowing she was expected downstairs. "I'll have to explain later."

"Can't wait to hear this one." Amber laughed.

"It's a good one," Sadie said. "I'll call you."

Ending the call, she gathered Coco in her arms, not bothering to place her in the tote bag, and headed downstairs to see what questions the detective had now. She found him at the end of the bar area, standing cautiously back from Paddy, who was enjoying a large bowl of whatever pigs tended to have for breakfast. The word *slop* ran through Sadie's mind, but she suspected the pub mascot dined on something more elegant. Or maybe not, she mused. Now curious, she made a mental note to ask Raff, who was busy stocking the bar in preparation for the day. But first she wanted to get whatever new interrogation was waiting over with.

"Good morning, Paddy," Sadie said, directing her statement toward the floor. She saw the pig was wearing a green sequined bow tie, which gave him a distinguished look. Paddy lifted his head to acknowledge her greeting.

"What can I do for you, Detective?" Sadie smiled, thinking somehow that a pleasant demeanor might lead to a shorter conversation.

"Where were you last night, Ms. Kramer?"

Oh, here we go, Sadie thought. *I know this conversation. Might as well get it out of the way.*

"I was here. I think we went over this. I had an order of fish and chips. I went to my room after that. I heard an argument outside."

"Were you alone?"

Sadie was tempted to tell him it was none of his business but knew this was just leading to the alibi portion of the questioning. She was also tempted to say she'd fallen into a fantastic romantic encounter shortly after her car broke down. She thought better of either of those responses and gave a straight answer.

"Yes, I was alone except for Coco here." She patted Coco, who was quite occupied watching Paddy eat.

The detective scribbled on his notepad. "So, you have no alibi."

There it is. "You could always ask Coco." Her quip was returned with something resembling a glower, which she supposed she deserved.

"She was definitely alone," Raff called over as he loaded bottles of beer into the refrigerated compartment behind the bar.

Sadie had two thoughts about that comment. On one hand, she was grateful to Raff for backing her up. On the other hand, did he have to be so certain that she *hadn't* fallen into a romantic tryst? She reviewed the pub scene from the night before. There had been one reasonably attractive man there at the pool table, though admittedly several decades too young for her. It was a strange mix of feelings that floated through her. She wasn't one to have that sort of adventure on a trip. Yet she didn't want to be considered someone who couldn't. That train of thought puzzled her more and more as the years went on. It was all a part of aging, she supposed.

"Anything else she can help you with, Detective?" Raff walked over to the end of the bar where Sadie and the detective stood, and Sadie couldn't help but wonder if he looked uneasy. Perhaps she was imagining it. But then again, maybe Raff was anxious to see the questioning end. Was the detective's presence making him uncomfortable?

Sadie glanced at the clock, noting that the pub would be opening soon. That might explain the bartender's eagerness to have the discussion end. It wouldn't be ideal to have a detective there when customers arrived. As it was, the news about Quinn would surely upset people if they hadn't already heard. Being a small town, she suspected many had. That was the way of small towns.

"That'll be all for now," Detective Ross said. He picked his hat up off the bar counter and put it on, resuming his Columbo look. "But I'll be back."

Yes, Sadie thought. *I'm sure you will.*

NINE

Feeling a need for air, Sadie waited long enough to be sure the detective was gone before wandering outside. The early-morning fog had lifted, replaced by sunshine, which seemed to lighten the serious atmosphere. Death had a way of spoiling a perfectly good day.

To the left of the market, she found a pathway with an access sign that indicated the way to the ocean. With Coco, who was not fond of walking on sand, curled up in one arm, she followed the trail through tall grasses until the gravel beneath her feet turned to sand and the path deposited her on the beach.

Sadie set to walking along the damp stretch of sand, letting her mind wander. At home in San Francisco, it was only a short drive to get to a beach, whether heading south along the coast or north across the Golden Gate Bridge into Marin County. Yet she rarely went. It was one of those things that tended to happen. Wherever home might be, it inspired the habit of staying home. Traveling brought with it a different state of mind, one that prompted exploring. This could be—but usually wasn't—a part of life at home. It was a different mindset.

The beach felt soothing to Sadie as she walked across the sand. Everything from the warmth of the sun to the sound of the crashing waves delighted her. In the distance, she could see a marina, set off behind a low rock jetty that held the waves at bay and allowed the water to be smooth enough for boats to attach to a narrow pier. It was far from the fancier marinas she'd seen in city areas, but it was a marina nonetheless, the kind one might find in a tiny coastal town.

As she walked, she thought about the pub and the interactions she'd seen there. She reevaluated the relationships she'd first assumed, realizing that all might not be as it seemed. There were clearly things going on behind the scenes, and they seemed to change from minute to minute.

As she approached the marina, she spotted Finnian waving to her. He stood on a small boat, one hand holding a cell phone to his ear. Sadie waved back with the one hand that wasn't holding Coco.

"Ahoy!" Sadie shouted as she drew near. She wasn't sure that was a proper greeting from shore to boat as opposed to the other way around, but it was what happened to come out of her mouth. Whether that was from watching too many pirate movies or from a book plot, she wasn't sure. There were few if any occasions in downtown San Francisco to shout "Ahoy!" as a greeting.

Finnian ended his call and slid his cell phone into his pocket as Sadie came down the pier. "What brings you down here to the boats?" he asked when she was close enough for conversation. Sadie thought he looked nervous. Had he been on a phone call he didn't want overheard?

"There aren't many boats here," Sadie said, observing empty slots along the side of the pier.

"Not enough people here in the area," Finnian said. "There's a bigger, fancier marina up the road about fifty miles. But this works for me." He patted the top of a small cabin. "Home sweet home."

"How long have you lived here?" Sadie asked.

"Not long. About a month." Finnian looked up the beach as if expecting someone. "I work remote. Gotta love the flexibility."

"It's a beautiful place to work," Sadie said, admiring the sunlight's reflection across the water. "Beats an inside job at a desk."

"You're right about that," Finnian said. "I've spent many hours working in a cubicle. Being outdoors fills the soul instead of the spreadsheets."

Sadie couldn't disagree with that. Her late husband had always preferred being out "in the field" as he called days away from his real estate development office. It was boring being indoors for hours at a time, days when planning was the focus rather than inspecting properties or meeting clients.

Sadie, on the other hand, enjoyed working inside. Her small office at the back of Flair had the feeling of a cozy retreat. She'd set it up that way from the start with a stylish desk, bookshelves, and a comfortable chair for times when she could go over invoices or fashion catalogs in her lap.

Then again, one of Sadie's comforts was knowing she was only one door away from her friend Matteo's gourmet chocolate shop. With fashion surrounding her in the boutique, a cozy office in the back, and unlimited access to chocolate next door, how could she possibly be uncomfortable?

"How are you finding life in Irishton?" Sadie wondered why she hadn't thought to ask that before. He seemed to always be on the outskirts of town activity rather than involved directly.

"It's okay," Finnian said as he checked to make sure the line securing his boat was tied off properly.

Sadie was surprised to hear the lack of enthusiasm in his answer but also thought it explained his limited involvement with the town. He was still settling in.

"I get tired of city life," Finnian said, answering a question she hadn't asked but wondered. "Sometimes I just want something different."

"I'm a city gal through and through," Sadie said. "I don't mind traveling and seeing how others live, but I'm comfortable with activity around me. Traffic sounds, conversations passing by on sidewalks, the aromas of food floating out of restaurants and cafés. There's always something greeting the senses."

Finnian brushed his hands against his jeans and looked out to sea. Sadie took it as a cue to head back to the pub. Thinking about city sounds reminded her she'd have a good amount of noise to look forward to today. And hopefully a bit of information.

Walking back to town, Sadie felt a familiar vibration in her pocket, and she pulled her phone out, expecting it to be Amber. Instead, she was surprised to see her favorite detective's name on the screen. She answered the call formally, as was their habit though they were far past the point of formality.

"Detective Broussard."

"Ms. Kramer."

"To what do I owe the pleasure of this call?" The teasing behind Sadie's words would be clear to Broussard, and that was fine. They'd long ago established the formal dance they did when entering phone conversations. Besides, she could already guess his reason for calling, and she soon learned she was right.

"The funniest thing just happened," Broussard began. "I called Flair to say hello and had an interesting conversation with Amber."

"Well, it couldn't have been too interesting. I barely had a chance to speak with her."

"So I understand. I believe she said your phone call was interrupted by... dare I say it... a detective."

"I suppose that's correct," Sadie said. "They seem to follow me everywhere." She chuckled, thrilled with her clever answer.

"I see," Broussard answered. "Does this mean I should be jealous? Or just worried you're in some kind of trouble again?"

Sadie smiled. "No need to be jealous. I'm only attracted to tall, handsome detectives, not short Columbo types. This one is the latter."

"Sounds like a generalization to me, the television detective reference."

"If the shoe fits." *Touché.* She amazed herself with witty retorts at times.

Even without being able to see through the phone, she was certain Broussard was smiling, but she also knew he was concerned, the degree of which depended on what Amber had said to him. Then again, how much could she have told him? Sadie hadn't even had a chance to say much to her before Detective Ross had interrupted.

"I'm not in any trouble, if that's what you're worried about. It just so happens someone passed away last night. Or this morning. I don't really know."

"Because you're not involved." It was clear from Broussard's tone that he hoped the statement was accurate.

"Not really. I mean no, not at all." Sadie winced, realizing her mistake at once. She should have opted for "Not at all" right off the bat.

"Who exactly passed away?"

"A business owner."

"Of what business?"

"A place called O'Paddy's Pub. It's named after a pig."

Broussard remained quiet at first. "A pub named after a pig. Well, why not?" Broussard finally said. "They say Portland is weird, right? That's a popular slogan? Keep Portland weird?"

Sadie hesitated, choosing her words carefully. "Yes, but... I'm not actually in Portland. I had a little mishap along the way. That is, my car did. So I ended up in a small town on the coast. The car's being repaired, but they've had to order a part. It seems I'm stuck here for a couple of days. It's not too bad. Odd little town but unique and entertaining."

"Are you at a decent hotel at least?"

Broussard's fatherly tone made her smile until she realized she'd have to explain her accommodations.

"Not exactly."

"What does that mean, not exactly?"

"There isn't a hotel here, so to speak."

"A motel then. Clean? Comfortable?"

"Not quite that," Sadie said. "The only overnight lodging is above a pub, on the second floor. O'Paddy's Pub."

"The one run by a pig..."

"*Named* after a pig. He doesn't run it." Sadie knew Broussard was teasing, but it didn't help when she was having trouble explaining the situation. "He's a very nice pig. Quite popular with customers. Coco seems fascinated with him. I'm not sure who runs the pub. It might have been the owner."

"Dare I ask why that last statement is in past tense?"

Oops. "Well, now that you ask, the owner of the pub happens to be the person who is deceased."

Broussard sighed. "Why does that not surprise me?"

"I don't think it's anything to worry about," Sadie said. "This didn't happen at the pub. It seems they found him at his home wherever that is."

"How do you know that? I mean, how did you find out?"

"I overheard it at the market this morning. Really, it's an everything store in my opinion: market, post office, probably a number of other things. There are only a few buildings in town. If you can call it a town, that is. Anyway, some guys were discussing it an aisle over. That's how I found out."

"Guys from the pub?"

Sadie thought back. "No. One was the guy who rescued me when my car broke down. Another was a local, the guy doing the car repair. A third was..."

"Was what?"

"Sort of odd. Gruff. I think he was from a neighboring town. A competitor, I guess."

"That could be suspicious," Broussard said. "I want you to be careful, Sadie. You do tend to get in the middle of these situations somehow. I suspect your curiosity has something to do with it. Let's hope this is a natural-causes situation and you stay clear of any kind of investigation."

"Why would the detective be asking questions if it's natural causes?" That was something Sadie had thought when she'd first seen Detective Ross.

"It could be just routine," Broussard said. "Making sure there's not a reason to suspect foul play."

"Or else they might suspect foul play and are trying to gather information before word gets around."

"Possibly. But either way, let's hope your car gets repaired quickly and you can continue on your way. For my peace of mind if not for yours."

"Sounds good to me," Sadie said. "I'll call you later and give you an update on the car situation so you won't worry. How does that sound?"

"Perfect. I'll look forward to it."

TEN

When Sadie returned to the pub, it was approaching noon. The popular spot had opened, and lunch activity was ramping up. Raff had gone home, leaving a day bartender in charge, an attractive young woman with blond hair pulled back in a ponytail. She sported—in Sadie's opinion—a bit too much makeup and a low-cut blouse that left little to the imagination. Sadie chastised herself quickly for being judgmental. It was likely a successful look for increasing tips and encouraging customers to linger. Besides, the woman had a right to dress any way she wanted.

The buzz of voices was noticeably more intense than it had been the day before, and Sadie realized the news of Quinn's death had spread quickly, just as she knew it would. The expressions on customer faces were a mix of shock and sadness. It was clear he was well-liked.

Although, thinking back to the conversation she'd overheard at the market earlier, there was at least one person who had some kind of grudge against the now-deceased bar owner. The statement "He probably had it coming" implied as much. And this was, if she remembered correctly, someone who had a competitive business up the road. Competition could breed cooperation, but it could also breed enemies.

Spotting Finnian at the bar, Sadie sauntered over and sat down next to him, Coco in her arms. She considered running up to get her tote bag for Coco to sit in. But looking around, she realized that not only was Paddy wandering the room freely but one customer had a beagle curled up on the floor by his chair and another had a parrot perched on his shoulder. Perhaps Paddy made the rules for O'Paddy's himself and had designated it an inclusive establishment. Whatever the case, she finally placed Coco on the barstool next to her, cautioning the pup to behave.

"Quite a morning," Finnian said, observing the room.

"So it seems," Sadie replied. "I can understand why so many people are upset. This pub is the center of the town."

Finnian nodded. "Everyone knew him."

"How big is this town anyway? What is the population?" Sadie had wondered this since arriving. There were only a few residential buildings in town. Others had to be hidden away from the highway.

"Barely two hundred," Finnian said. "Not a big pool of suspects."

Sadie perked up at the word *suspects*. "Does this mean they've determined foul play? Detective Ross was here earlier asking questions."

"Not that I know of. I haven't heard anything. That's just my opinion that there might be something fishy here. Quinn looked perfectly fine yesterday. It's hard to believe he would suddenly pass away."

"People do have heart attacks, you know." Sadie contemplated a variety of causes that could be natural. Or accidental, for that matter. "What about drugs? Did he have a problem? Could it be an overdose or something like that?"

"I don't think so," Finnian said. "Quinn seemed pretty straight in that regard. Maybe a beer or two on occasion, but he wasn't even a regular at his own pub. I'd be surprised if he had anything to do with drugs."

Lost in her thoughts, the arrival of the day bartender in front of her took her by surprise. Now that she was close, it was clear the young woman had been crying. Perhaps the makeup was an attempt to cover this.

"Ready for lunch?" The bartender set a small menu on the counter.

Sadie noticed Finnian step away and head for the front door. That sparked her curiosity, but she turned her attention back to the issue at hand. "Yes, that sounds like a great idea. I skipped breakfast with everything going on. What do you suggest?"

The woman tapped the menu, which turned out to be only a small sampling of what the regular menu had contained the night before. "We have limited choices today so the kitchen can prep for the corned beef and cabbage feast tomorrow."

"That's right," Sadie said. "Saint Patrick's Day is tomorrow." Thinking of the festivities to come, she was almost glad her car had broken down. Almost. There was still the little situation with the owner's death. Talk about being in the wrong place at the wrong time.

"Yes, Saint Patrick's Day." The bartender's eyes filled with tears. "My favorite holiday. And now... Oh, it doesn't matter. What can I get you? My name is Janna, by the way."

Sadie looked over the abbreviated menu quickly, her mind more occupied with the young woman's distress than with a lunch order. Still, she made herself focus on the printed options and made a choice.

"The clam chowder sounds good. And an order of fries, thanks." Coco lifted her head from the next seat and yipped, having recognized the word *fries*. That brought a smile to Janna's face, and Sadie was glad to see her have a light moment in view of the difficult day.

"Yes, Coco," Sadie said as Janna walked away to place the order. "You can have a fry or two. But not too many." She felt movement to her other side and turned to see Finnian sliding back onto his seat.

"Getting something to eat?" Sadie said. She handed him the menu, but he placed it in a metal holder without looking at it.

"I'm not hungry," Finnian said. "I just ran into Grady."

"Oh!" Sadie looked around but saw no sign of the mechanic. "Perhaps my car is ready?"

Finnian shook his head. "I wouldn't count on it. But I did get an update on Quinn. It seems he died from a head injury, blunt force trauma."

"My, how terrible!"

"It gets worse," Finnian continued. "There was nothing near him that could have caused those injuries. Meaning he didn't trip and fall."

Sadie knew where this was going. An accidental death was looking less likely. Which meant the most likely scenario was murder.

ELEVEN

It was no surprise when Detective Ross came around again, asking questions and searching the premises. Employees were asked to stay, patrons were asked to leave, and Sadie seemed to fall somewhere in the middle. At the detective's request, she opened her room up for inspection. After all, there was nothing much for him to find except gourmet dog treats, reading material, and whimsical pajamas. Still, he made quite a show of sorting through everything from her mystery paperbacks to her unmentionables, searching for who knows what.

It occurred to her briefly that he might be showing extra enthusiasm just to annoy her, but she hadn't been that flippant when she met him earlier, at least not for her. She'd been known to annoy many a detective with her tendency toward snarky comments and responses. But not in this case. He was undoubtedly just being cautious, not wanting to overlook anything.

Detective Ross finished looking through Sadie's room and moved on to searching those that were unoccupied. That made sense to Sadie. She would have done the same. What better place to hide incriminating evidence than a vacant room? And there were only three other rooms, two for guests plus the one Quinn used for his office, which Detective Ross saved for last.

Sadie did her best to peek in as he thumbed through papers and opened filing cabinet drawers. But Detective Ross took no time closing the door once he saw Sadie observing, and she soon was alone in the hallway.

Footsteps on the stairs preceded Janna's appearance. "Can we open again yet? Customers are getting restless outside, and we're losing money by the minute."

Even knowing she was alone, Sadie looked over her shoulder to see if the question was directed at her. Why would Janna be asking *her* if the pub could open? Then again, there was no one else there to ask. She'd won the question by default.

"I can ask Detective Ross. He's in Quinn's office." Sadie pointed to the closed door. "I'll find out for you." *And maybe get a glimpse of whatever's going on in there.*

"You know what? Don't bother." Janna turned back toward the stairs. "I'm just going to open. He can get mad if he wants. We need the business. And there's too much to do to prepare for tomorrow. Thank heavens this didn't happen then."

Sadie watched Janna disappear down the stairs. The rushed manner of her words seemed odd, like the chattering people tend to do at times when they're nervous or distraught. Perhaps Janna was both. It was certainly understandable.

Before she had time to ponder this further, the door to Quinn's office opened and Detective Ross stepped out.

"You're still standing here. I didn't expect to see you."

"Where did you expect me to be?"

Detective Ross frowned, a look that did him no favors when combined with his odd attire and abrupt manner of speaking. "Anywhere but here. I thought closing the door might make it clear that I plan to investigate on my own."

"Oh, it did make that clear," Sadie said. After all, she knew what a closed door meant. She had just chosen to ignore it.

"Then why are you still here?"

"I was thinking," Sadie said for lack of a better explanation. "And then the bartender came up to ask if she could open the pub again, which she decided to do on her own instead of waiting to find out."

"That's fine," Detective Ross said. "This isn't the crime scene anyway."

Somehow Sadie was disappointed that he wasn't a little more perturbed at the place reopening without his personal approval. Yet she was delighted with his wording. Stating that this "wasn't the crime scene" served as confirmation that there *was* a crime scene. Although she already knew that from talking to Finnian, it felt more official to hear it from the detective. This was progress.

Detective Ross headed downstairs. Sadie followed him, and Coco followed her. As they reached the bottom of the stairs, Paddy joined them, although trailing well behind. This resembled a parade with everyone keeping up except one straggler at the end. Of course, it wasn't Paddy's fault. This was simply the nature of a pig in a parade.

Janna was already busy behind the bar, more with food orders than with drinks, though a few mugs of beer dotted the counter. It was late afternoon already, and potato skins and buffalo wings appeared to be in high demand. Sadie approved, having always been a big believer in snacking. The concept of three meals a day was fine for those who liked order and routine. For Sadie, life was intended to be an adventure, one that included snacks.

With that thought in mind, she veered off and made her way to the bar, taking a place at the end. Coco and Paddy headed for a corner of the room. Paddy, ever the consummate host, pulled a blanket from a low shelf and snuffled it around with his snout until it formed a cozy resting place. The two settled in side by side, eyeing each other with the cautious optimism typical of new friendships.

"What can I get you?" Janna said. "Appetizers are half-price right now for happy hour."

Sadie nodded, now understanding the sudden flow of such items from the kitchen. Everyone loved a bargain, herself included. She ordered mozzarella sticks, which landed in front of her quickly, accompanied by marinara sauce for dipping.

"Good choice," an approaching voice said. Grady leaned across the bar counter and called in an order for the same. Janna responded with a thumbs-up as a sign that she'd heard him.

"I don't suppose you've come to tell me my car's ready." Even as she spoke, Sadie realized that she half hoped he would say no. Things were beginning to get interesting around Irishton. Therefore, she wasn't at all disappointed at his answer.

"Not yet, I'm afraid," Grady said. "Sorry to disappoint you. It seems you're stuck here for Saint Patrick's Day. However, they say the part will be here the following morning, so you'll only have to put up with us for another, oh, forty-eight hours or so."

Sadie dipped a mozzarella stick into the marinara sauce. "As it turns out, I can't think of a more entertaining place to be for this holiday. I'm looking forward to it." *And especially to finding out what happened to the poor soul who owned this establishment*, she added silently as she took a bite of the melted cheese. She sighed and closed her eyes at the exceptionally good appetizer.

"I see your guard dog has made a friend," Grady said, observing the duo curled up on the blanket.

"Yes, she has." Sadie looked down at the petite Yorkie now curled up against Paddy's side. "They seem to have hit it off quite well."

Grady thanked Janna as his order landed in front of him along with a beer, apparently another telepathic beverage order like the ones she'd seen the day before.

"No green beer?" Sadie asked.

"Tomorrow," Grady said as he raised the glass of golden lager. "It wouldn't be Saint Patrick's Day without it." He took a decent gulp and set his glass back down. "They'll fix it up tonight in a keg with injectable dye."

"Deep in thought?" Finnian joined them, arriving slightly out of breath.

"Just contemplating 'injectable dye,'" Sadie said. "It sounds rather sinister."

"It's just food coloring," Grady said. He took a bite of mozzarella. "Nothing to worry about. We have it every year."

"I wonder if that's something to worry about." Sadie pointed to the door by the dartboard, where Detective Ross was just stepping out, a plastic bag in each hand. Finnian followed her gesture, and Sadie thought she saw a glimmer of concern cross his face, though it disappeared quickly.

Sadie strained to see the bags' contents. "Must be some sort of evidence."

Grady coughed unexpectedly, and Sadie looked at him.

"Are you okay?"

Grady nodded. "Yes, I just swallowed wrong. Serves me right for eating these too quickly." He gestured to his basket of mozzarella sticks.

"I understand," Sadie said, waving her hand in the air casually. "I do that too sometimes." *Especially if something makes me nervous. Like a detective finding evidence.*

TWELVE

As happy hour grew happier, Sadie removed herself from both the activity and conflicting feelings she was getting from local characters. She gathered Coco into her arms, retrieved a leash from upstairs, and headed out to walk through the town that wasn't a town.

The few buildings she'd frequented since arriving were situated close together. While the gas station, market, and pub formed the main part of the town, a few smaller structures spread outward along the main street from there in addition to residences on side streets. A weathered building that was not much more than a shack appeared to be a former art gallery. A driftwood sign bearing the words IRISHTON GALLERY hung above the doorway. The interior was empty except for two chairs lying on their sides. A metal newspaper rack stood not far from a park area with a rustic bench and an indeterminable number of weed varieties. Beside one side street that could almost—but not quite —be called paved, a row of mailboxes stood at attention side by side as if hoping someone might stop by to say hello. Sadie accommodated that thought by patting each lonely metal box while Coco stood by, watching with either curiosity or envy.

As she walked, Sadie debated the characters she'd met since

arriving in the funny town. Finnian had been kind enough to stop and offer help when her car broke down. And he managed to check in to see how she was doing whenever he stopped by O'Paddy's.

Grady also struck her as an upright fellow, though she was taken aback by his odd reaction to Detective Ross removing items from the back room.

Rafferty seemed to keep to himself. Still, she was sure he was the one who had stepped outside to break up the heated discussion. Did he simply not want the commotion happening outside the business establishment? Or did he have some personal reason to break it up?

Sadie took a seat on the bench and was running those thoughts through her head when a speeding vehicle drew her attention to the road. A metallic-blue truck rushed by, followed by the sound of screeching tires. Sadie braced herself for crunching metal but heard nothing more than an engine idling in the distance. Walking to the side of the road, she could see the truck had stopped in front of the pub. Drew jumped out of the truck and entered the building.

Tugging on Coco's leash to encourage a faster pace, Sadie hurried toward the bar, eager to see what kind of drama was about to unfold. Before she even reached the pub, Drew and Janna both emerged, a heated debate in progress that became clear enough to hear as Sadie came close.

"You had no right to do that!" Janna yelled.

Drew took several steps away, then reversed them, stopping eye to eye with Janna, hands on his hips. "That's where we disagree, little lady," he shouted.

Oh, no, no, no, Sadie thought. *Do not call her "little lady."* Not only was it condescending, it was surely not going to earn him any brownie points.

"Do *not* call me that," Janna said, earning a huge dose of Sadie's respect. She'd always admired someone who could stand up to a bully.

"What do you say we go discuss this at my place?" Drew reached out to grab Janna's arm, but she ducked and stepped away.

"Absolutely not!" She crossed her arms, her hands squeezing her elbows.

Drew reached for her again just as the front door to the pub burst open.

"Leave her alone!" Grady shouted. "You don't own her or anyone else in this town."

"Who are you to tell me what I do or don't own, you little grease monkey?" He shoved Grady's shoulders with both hands. Grady stumbled back but recovered. He took a swing that barely connected as Drew bolted to the side. Drew then countered with a swing of his own, this one landing squarely on Grady's face, sending him down to the ground.

"Grady!" Janna and Sadie both ran to help, Coco trotting along just behind.

A new sound of tires squealing joined the frantic scene. A car door slammed, and Detective Ross's voice barked orders. "Break it up! You hear me? Now!"

Sadie was rather impressed with the authority the detective was able to manifest so suddenly. Perhaps she had underestimated him earlier.

"What seems to be the problem *this* time, Drew?" Detective Ross said. "And why is it every time I turn around, you're involved in some kind of fight? Stay right here." He pointed to the ground and then turned away to check on Grady, who was struggling to stand up.

The detective reached out a strong arm and grabbed Grady's hand. Sadie and Janna helped steady him as he accepted the help. Soon he was standing, one hand on his face. Janna gently lifted his hand away from his cheek. A bruise was already forming around one eye.

"You're going to have quite a shiner there," Detective Ross said.

"I'll get some ice." Janna disappeared into the pub.

"Courtesy of the jerk over there," Grady said, pointing to Drew. "I just wish I'd landed the first punch better."

"Or at all," Drew said, smirking.

"That's enough out of you," Detective Ross said. "Both of you. This is a place of business, not a junior high locker room. What started it? Or I suppose I should say, what started it *this* time?"

"He threw her drink away," Grady said, nodding toward Drew.

Detective Ross scratched his head. "This ruckus is over a spilled drink?"

"Not a spilled drink." Grady said. "Janna planned to stay to help decorate for tomorrow. But Drew seems to think he runs other people's lives, so he tossed her drink in the trash and told her she wasn't staying."

"That's right," Janna said, returning with an ice pack, which she handed to Grady. "I'd just finished my shift. Raff took over for the evening. I planned to stay, have a drink, hang some streamers and shamrocks from the ceiling. You know, get ready for tomorrow. It's the busiest day of the year for us."

Detective Ross turned to Drew. "I don't see why there's a problem here. Janna can do whatever she pleases when she gets off work."

Drew shrugged. "Fine."

"You need to stop bossing people around," Grady said. "You act like people are your property. They aren't." He pressed the ice to his face and winced.

"Why don't you all go inside," Detective Ross suggested. "I'll have a little chat here with Drew about minding his own business."

"You're letting him go?" Drew protested. "He swung at me first!"

"Really?" Detective Ross's tone was nothing short of exasperation. "Now we're going for elementary school tactics instead of junior high locker room? The old 'he started it' routine?"

Again Drew shrugged. Janna rolled her eyes and helped Grady toward the pub.

Sadie, for lack of any other clear option, tugged gently on Coco's leash and followed the others inside.

THIRTEEN

oco's head swiveled as soon as they entered the pub, and Sadie's curiosity perked up. Was it possible Coco was looking for Paddy? The two had gotten along well when they shared the blanket together earlier. It seemed an unlikely friendship—a potbellied pig and a Yorkie—but, from outward appearances, this was the case.

Sure enough, Paddy moseyed over from the pool table as soon as he spotted Coco. Having decided by now that O'Paddy's was half pub, half free-range farm, Sadie unclipped Coco's leash and let the two run off together, though "running off" was more fitting to Coco's pace while "plodding along" was a better description of Paddy's forward motion. In any case, the two met up at the blanket area and settled in.

"Back again?" Raff said as Sadie took a seat at the bar counter. He placed a cocktail napkin in front of her. "What'll it be? How about a pineapple-and-lime mocktail?"

"That sounds delicious," Sadie said. "Am I correct in assuming that green beer will be flowing here tomorrow?"

Raff laughed. "I'd say you can count on green everything. We do it up right for this holiday. It'll be crowded too."

"It sounds like fun."

"It will be," Janna said half-heartedly. She slid onto a barstool next to Sadie. "Music, games, beer, refreshments, noise and more noise."

Sadie looked at Janna sympathetically. "I know this is a hard time for you. I'm sorry."

"Thanks," Janna said, her voice quivering. "I loved my uncle so much. He always took care of me. And now I'll take care of O'Paddy's, just as he wanted me to do."

Sadie looked between Janna and Raff. "Won't his death put a damper on the celebration tomorrow?"

Janna shook her head. "No. It'll be okay. He would have wanted the pub to be open."

"Look at it this way," Raff said, attempting to explain what would normally seem like a strange situation. "The tradition of an Irish wake goes way back. It's not just about mourning the death of a person. It's also about celebrating their life. Irish wakes can seem strange to people because there's a mix of sadness and cele-bration."

"Even pranks," Grady said. He took a seat next to Sadie and accepted a fresh ice pack from Raff. "Not so much now, but in the old days. My grandfather used to tell me he and a friend would hide under the bed the body was on and shake it to scare those paying their respects."

"That would give me the creeps!" Sadie exclaimed. Yet she understood the idea of adding levity to a somber situation. Different nationalities and cultures had different ways of marking life events.

"So having the pub open is not being disrespectful," Raff said. "It's a way of celebrating Quinn's life. The fact that it's Saint Patrick's Day just makes it even more of a party."

"Quinn would have liked that," Grady said. "A good old-fash-ioned Irish wake but in a pub with all the trappings of the holiday. It doesn't get any more Irish than that."

Raff poured a shot of whiskey and placed it in front of Grady.

"And here's a good old-fashioned remedy for that injury you're nursing there."

"Thanks." Grady picked up the glass with his free hand while the other held the ice pack against his face. He downed the shot quickly and ordered another.

Sadie looked around, confirmed that Coco was still doing fine in Paddy's corner, and turned back to Raff, Grady, and Janna. "So, what's the deal with this guy Drew?" Although she posed the question to them all, she watched for an answer from Janna in particular.

"It's my fault," Janna said.

"No," Sadie replied immediately. "It's never your fault when someone bullies you."

"Exactly," Grady said. "I keep telling her that."

Grady's comment reminded Sadie that he clearly had protective instincts where Janna was concerned. Maybe chivalry wasn't a thing of the past despite how things seemed these days.

"I made the mistake of dating him." Janna sighed in the way people do when admitting something they regret. "I don't know why. I happened to be up the road at his bar one day. He introduced himself to me, and I went out with him a few times."

"Then she got smart," Grady quipped.

Janna nodded. "I told him we needed to stop seeing each other, that I just wasn't interested."

"I'm guessing he didn't take it well," Sadie said.

"Not at all," Janna said. "He started coming down here all the time, wouldn't accept that I didn't want to see him."

"Bruised ego," Sadie mused.

"Something like that." Janna picked up a cocktail napkin and dabbed her eyes. "Anyway, I couldn't get away from him because this is my job. I can't just leave whenever he comes around. Quinn would always stick up for me when he was here. He'd throw Drew out. Or at least he'd try to. A couple of times he had to call the police to have him removed."

"That must have been unpleasant, having him show up here at your place of employment," Sadie said.

Grady smacked his free hand on that bar counter. "That's one way to put it."

Sadie tried to determine whether Grady's harsh reaction was just a gesture of agreement or if it was anger. She thought back to the argument she'd overheard outside the pub at night. Was Grady one of the men she'd heard? Had Drew been the other? She looked at Raff and then back to Grady. Had Raff been telling Grady and Drew to leave? Which would mean Drew and Grady might have been arguing about Janna.

The plot thickens, Sadie thought. There was a lot that needed to be explained. A few things were certain though. The owner of O'Paddy's was dead, Saint Patrick's Day was only one day away, and there were multiple suspects. Which was when it occurred to Sadie that she might need to visit the bar up the road.

Fourteen

Sadie finished her drink, making a point to turn conversation to light banter, which proved to be easy. No one wanted to dwell on Quinn's death or Drew and Grady's fight or anything other than looking forward to the next day's holiday activities. This served her purpose, which had become focused. She knew not to take anyone at face value, no matter how friendly they seemed. There was a current of something running beneath all the pub goings-on. It was just a matter of finding out what it was.

Sadie fetched Coco from the corner, apologizing to Paddy for gathering Coco up the same way a parent might apologize to a child's friend for needing to call her own child home. That caused her to chuckle. If she'd been told before that she'd be apologizing to a pig for anything, she wouldn't have believed it. Yet here she was doing exactly that.

With Coco in tow, she retired to her room upstairs and tried to come up with a game plan. She knew what she wanted to do. She'd had plenty of time to observe the activity at O'Paddy's. It was time to check out the other watering hole. The problem was, with her car broken down, how would she get to the other one? It couldn't be a ride with anyone from O'Paddy's. If she got too close to the truth, she could end up in danger herself. And she wasn't about to hitchhike. That was an activity of her youth, back before things either became more dangerous or she simply grew into being more sensible.

What did that leave as a possible mode of transportation "up the road" as they called it? There wasn't a bus line she could hop. And if there had been a car rental place in town, she wouldn't be stuck in Irishton to begin with. Asking Detective Ross was out of the question. He'd be the first one to refuse to take her.

Finnian. That's who she could ask. If she phrased it nonchalantly, maybe he would take her up to Drew's Place and she could see what was going on up there.

Sadie fixed a bowl of Coco's favorite dinner and set it in the travel palace. While the pup ate, she washed her face and put on fresh makeup, preparing for her trip to check out Drew's bar. She changed into warmer clothes to accommodate the evening temperatures and, once Coco finished dinner, settled the dog into her tote bag and headed downstairs in search of Finnian. Not seeing him in the pub, she tried the market but to no avail. Discouraged, she took a seat at a picnic table outside and debated her options. Walking was out of the question. Hadn't someone said it was "a ways" up the road? Which, for a coast highway, couldn't be less than a mile, and that was about all she could manage, especially at the late hour. Besides, how would she get back if she was alone?

She was beginning to wish once again that she was comfortably housed in Portland as she had expected to be by now. She'd have a huge stack of new books to read and probably room service to go along with it. That thought made her realize she hadn't eaten anything since earlier. Just as she was debating going back to the pub for an order of fish and chips or perhaps their Irish stew, a familiar car pulled up.

"Broken down again but not with your car this time?" Finnian's joking tone put her at ease. Now she just had to find a way to convince him to take her to Drew's Place without having it sound too suspicious.

"Just bored," Sadie said. "I needed to get out. There's just nowhere to go. No offense to the town."

"I don't disagree with you," Finnian said. "I'd tell you to go check out the pub, but you're staying there, so that would be pointless."

Sadie sighed, hoping to give the impression of restlessness. "There must be somewhere else to go around here, isn't there? You know the area." She waited, leaving the veiled suggestion hanging in the air.

"Well," Finnian said. "There's that place up the road that Drew runs. It's nothing special, but I was headed up there anyway if you want to tag along. About all I can say about it is that it isn't here."

"Not here sounds good to me." Sadie hoped she sounded nonchalant. This was going exactly the way she'd hoped.

"I have time to kill," Finnian said. "Why don't I give you a ride up there? I assume you have your guard dog with you?"

That was the offer she'd been hoping to get.

"Yes." Sadie patted her tote bag. "One guard dog present and accounted for." She stood and hoisted the straps of her tote bag over her shoulder. "That would be wonderful," she said as she climbed in his car. "I'd welcome a change of scenery about now."

"I'm sure you would," Finnian said.

The drive to Drew's Place took about fifteen minutes, perhaps not even that long. A much smaller building than O'Paddy's, it looked semibusy from the outside. Half a dozen cars dotted the small parking lot, most parked along the front of the building. Finnian parked alongside a black SUV that looked oddly out of place among the other relatively basic cars. Sadie noticed Finnian frown at it as they walked by.

Rock music flowed from the door as they approached, hitting a disturbing volume once they stepped inside. Sadie remembered the thrill in her younger years of having to shout over music in nightclubs in order to be heard. Something about that energy had been exciting back then. Forty years later, it was only annoying. Still, she was where she wanted to be, inside the establishment of the gruff guy who'd been hanging around O'Paddy's and bullying Janna.

Finnian offered to buy her a drink, but she declined. Not only did she wish to remain clearheaded but she also didn't expect to stay long. After checking to be sure she'd be fine on her own for a few minutes, Finnian stepped outside, this time leaving through a side door. She noticed a man at the bar stand and follow him out, which she found curious.

Sadie looked around, sizing the place up. A few small tables filled the claustrophobic space, and a microphone stand stood in one corner of the room, signaling the potential for live music, though the current music was through the sound system. There was no room for a pool table. She figured the bar survived on locals needing a place to go without going anywhere at all. It was clean enough, but it lacked the personality of O'Paddy's. It was simply a roadside bar, a very small one at that.

Whether she expected to find Drew or not, he was nowhere to be seen. That was a relief as he might have wondered what had brought her up. Using boredom as an excuse might have worked, but fortunately, she didn't have to rely on it.

Finnian returned within minutes and asked if she wanted to stay longer. The man who'd left just behind him did not return. She looked around, then shook her head. Not only did she not want to inconvenience him, but there was also nothing left to see.

Back in the parking lot, Finnian held the door open for Sadie, a touch that she appreciated. As he circled the front of the car to get to the driver's side, she looked around. A few more cars had left, including the black SUV. There was nothing else of note. Drew's Place appeared to be as uninteresting as it could be, which might have been exactly what she wanted to find out.

Arriving back at O'Paddy's, Sadie thanked Finnian for the ride and started for the front door to the pub. As she neared the entrance, the sound of music inside seemed to weigh on top of the loud music she'd just been exposed to at Drew's Place. She decided to go around the building and use the back staircase to get to her room.

It had grown dark by this time, and she stepped carefully to avoid gravel or rocks on the ground. Which was how she ended up surprising Grady and Janna—not to mention herself—as she rounded the back corner of the building and found them in a passionate embrace.

An attempt to draw back unnoticed failed, as they saw her before she could retreat. They stepped away from each other quickly.

"Oh!" Sadie exclaimed. "I'm so sorry to have frightened you. I just thought I'd avoid the noise in the pub by coming around here to the rear entrance."

"Exactly what we were thinking," Janna said. "It's so hard to hear each other inside. This is the easiest place to have a conversation." She turned to Grady. "Right?"

Grady ran his fingers through his hair. "Um, yeah, exactly. It's just too noisy in there, especially this late at night."

"Indeed," Sadie said. "And it will be even noisier tomorrow night, I bet."

"Absolutely," Janna said. "And not only at night. You can count on Saint Patrick's Day to be crazy from the moment we open the doors until we close."

"Rowdy might be a better term," Grady said.

Sadie looked forward to that. Not only would the commotion be entertaining but it might be conducive to finding Quinn's killer. A little ruckus combined with some celebratory holiday imbibing could loosen things up enough to shake a few leafy details from the proverbial tree. In fact, she was counting on it. Expecting the unexpected was always intriguing if not telling. Just as rounding the corner of the pub had been.

"I'm looking forward to it!" Sadie said as she reached the bottom of the stairs.

Bidding them good night, she climbed the stairs and retired to her room. She took Coco out of the tote bag and got her settled in her crate, refilling the water bowl and setting a treat on the velvet pillow. This was her version of turndown service. After all, they were traveling, and Coco always deserved the best treatment. If hotels could offer that to guests, she could offer it to Coco.

Trying to ignore the music floating up from downstairs, Sadie changed into her favorite pink flamingo pajamas, slid into bed, and tried to read. But, try as she might, she could not get her mind to focus on the story. Images from the day haunted her: the odd ambiance inside Drew's Place, the way Finnian had slipped out the side door, the black SUV in the parking lot, the fight between Drew and Grady, and the passionate entanglement of Janna and Grady behind the pub. What on earth was going on in Irishton?

FIFTEEN

A gentle scraping noise woke Sadie the following morning, and she sat up, trying to figure out what she was hearing. Coco was awake but appeared to have just opened her eyes. She was as curious about the odd sound as Sadie was.

After several more scrapes and some searching around the room, it became clear that the noise was coming from the door. Uncertain what to do after the events of the night before, Sadie called through the door to see who was on the other side but received no answer. She kept the door chained but opened it far enough to peek outside. Seeing no one in the hallway, she started to close the door, but a huffing sound caused her to look down, where she found the source of the noise.

"Paddy! What are you doing here?" Sadie exclaimed. "You know someone is going to have to come up and retrieve you." As soon as the words left her mouth, Sadie realized how silly she must sound, reprimanding a pig. Besides, the pub was Paddy's home. Certainly he could go wherever he wanted.

Coco, hearing Sadie's voice, stood up and crossed the room to see what was going on. Upon seeing Paddy at the door, Coco became animated, yipping with delight at the sight of her new friend.

Sadie ran a hand across her forehead, trying to make sense of the situation. Was this really how she was starting her day? Standing in the doorway of an upstairs lodging room in an old Irish pub, wearing pink flamingo pajamas and talking to a potbellied pig? Even Amber, who knew her tendency to fall into strange situations, would have trouble understanding.

That thought reminded Sadie to give Amber a call later once the boutique was open. Even hearing the most boring of stories—what items were ready to be marked down, which display units needed dusting—would be a decent diversion from the events in Irishton.

"Come on in, Paddy." Sadie stood back and gestured to the center of the room. "I'll take you back downstairs when I go down for breakfast if they haven't come up to get you by then."

Paddy sauntered in, looked around, and after a failed attempt to fit inside Coco's crate, plopped down on the floor. Coco, being a true host, took a place next to the visiting pig.

"Great, just great," Sadie muttered as she rifled through her clothes, looking to put together an outfit appropriate for the holiday. She'd brought a soft green mohair sweater from Flair specifically for the occasion, which she paired with black slacks. She was certain she'd be overdressed for the pub crowd, but at least she'd be wearing the correct color. She didn't miss those schooldays of getting pinched for not wearing green on the holiday in question.

Always a fan of accessories, she'd made sure to bring dangling shamrock earrings along with a necklace to match. Bright green bangle bracelets added even more color to the outfit, and sparkly gold flats completed the look. She checked herself in the mirror, pleased with the overall effect.

Coco and Paddy seemed pleased as well, and Sadie awarded each one a small treat as thanks for their support.

A voice accompanied a knock on the door, and Sadie could

hear Raff calling for Paddy. She opened the door and pointed to the friends on the floor.

"I'm guessing this is who you're looking for? I was planning to bring him down in a few minutes. He was... I guess you could say knocking on the door this morning."

Raff nodded. "Yes, he does that when he wants to go out or come in. He's very well trained, just as you might expect a dog to be."

"So I see." Sadie took a look at Paddy, seeing him from a new perspective. "That's quite remarkable, now that I think about it. I don't think most people know that a pig could be a pet. I rather like the idea." Sadie contemplated that for all of five seconds before vetoing the thought. A San Francisco penthouse apartment was hardly the right environment for a pig. Just the number of trips in and out, even with the express elevator, made the idea impractical.

"I'll take him downstairs," Raff said. "I need to get him ready for the day anyway. He's something of a celebrity every March 17."

"I imagine so," Sadie said. "Especially with his name being what it is. You'll be working tonight, I imagine."

"Today and tonight," Raff said. "I'll be pulling a double. So will Janna. It's all hands on deck today."

"Yes, I'm sure you'll be busy. I can always help if you need an extra hand. I've done some restaurant work before." *Decades before*, Sadie reminded herself. *But who's counting?* And help was help in any case. Besides, she just might see something illuminating by being out on the floor.

Raff nodded. "We just might take you up on that. We were counting on Quinn to help, but..."

"I understand," Sadie said, although there was much left to understand.

Raff gestured to Paddy to follow him, and amazingly, Paddy did just that. Coco let out a sad yip at seeing Paddy depart, but

Sadie assured her he'd be downstairs later when they went into the pub.

"Time to find something for breakfast, Coco. For both of us." She filled a bowl with Coco's special blend and set it in front of her. Once Coco had finished, she clipped the green leash on the petite pup and headed to the market. Certainly the bakery section had something calling her name.

Sixteen

An air of celebration filled the market that was not present when Sadie was there before. The bakery section's freshly baked treats all featured an Irish theme: sugar cookies shaped like shamrocks, cupcakes with a pot of gold on top, and frosted donuts with green and gold sprinkles. Sparkling green shamrock-shaped lights hung in scalloped form across the front window, and Susanna at the front counter wore a tall sequined leprechaun hat. Celtic music played on the sound system. Overall, the atmosphere was more like a party than a small-town market.

Locals gathered outside, all wearing some type of holiday garb or accessories, each looking more cheerful than the next.

An elderly man in a green-and-gold flannel shirt greeted Sadie and Coco as they approached. "Top o' the morning to you!"

Sadie returned the greeting, somehow pulling a line from the memory of a school skit years ago. "And the rest of the morning to you!"

A tall woman of slender physique sported a white blouse with a lovely green overdress, attire fitting an Irish festival, just right for Saint Patrick's Day in the small coastal town of Irishton.

Several children played tag, chasing each other around in

circles while holding "pots of gold" similar to trick-or-treat pump-kins. Each wore a headband with wiggling shamrock antennae.

A familiar voice called out to Sadie. "Now you'll see how Saint Patrick's Day should be celebrated!" Finnian stood near the market doorway, leaning on a post. He wore a green jacket, white shirt, jeans, and held a mug of what Sadie felt quite sure was Irish coffee. And why not? No one was going anywhere that day. They were right where they wanted to be.

Detective Ross was absent, but Sadie was certain he'd be around at some point during the day, seeing as the mystery of Quinn's death had yet to be solved. And with a town event that was sure to bring everyone out, possibly including the killer, he wasn't likely to miss it.

Sadie purchased not one but two frosted donuts with the idea of saving one for later. At least that was her intention, though she'd never been known to have much willpower when it came to donuts or any sweets for that matter. She settled down at a small table not far from Finnian and enjoyed a cup of coffee along with her breakfast sweets.

"Any word on your car?" Finnian asked. "Are you going to be able to escape this crazy little town soon?"

That threw Sadie off for a moment. She realized she'd become so entranced with the town and people that she'd almost forgotten about the car repair. She also hadn't gotten an update from Grady.

A car pulled up in front of the pub, and Janna jumped out. Apron in hand, she walked to the pub's front door and entered as the car drove off.

"Sadie?" Finnian's voice reached her, and she realized he'd been speaking to her without her answering in turn.

"I'm sorry," Sadie said quickly. "I was just noticing Janna arriving for work. It's going to be a busy day over there. I told Raff I'd be willing to help if they needed me. What were you saying?"

"I just asked if you knew when your car would be ready." Finnian took a sip of his coffee.

Sadie shook her head. "I haven't talked to Grady. I imagine it'll be ready tomorrow. That's when he expects the part to come in. I should be on my way by midafternoon, I imagine. Luckily, I only have a few hours to drive."

This was reassuring, the thought she only had a short drive as opposed to an all-day trip. Not only did it mean she'd be in Portland by nightfall, it also meant she'd have time to see how the Quinn situation developed before she hit the road. Hopefully there'd be updates by then.

Finnian downed the rest of his Irish coffee and set the mug in a bus tray that had been placed outside in anticipation of the crowd. "I'd better get down to the marina. I wouldn't want any leprechauns causing trouble while I wasn't looking."

"Very smart of you," Sadie said. She followed the statement with a bite of donut as Finnian sauntered toward the beach.

"He's a smart guy," Grady said as he walked up. "And by the way, your car should be ready by early tomorrow afternoon." He took a seat beside Sadie and reached down to pet Coco, who was currently fascinated with the bobbing shamrocks on the toddlers' heads. "They confirmed that the part would arrive early in the morning. We'll have you on your way in no time."

Sadie held up a finger, her mouth still occupied with the donut. "Great news, Grady," she said once she was able to speak. "I appreciate it, though I must say this detour has been anything but boring. For a small town, a lot seems to happen here."

"Not usually as much as this," Grady said, shaking his head. "I wish we knew what happened to Quinn."

"Maybe Detective Ross will find out soon," Sadie offered. "That's his job. This is his area, right?"

Grady nodded. "Yep. He's the only officer around these immediate parts. Makes sense, seeing as the population is so small. Most days, even weeks, there's nothing going on. He's probably glad to have something to occupy his time."

"I guess this week makes up for the slow times." Sadie took

another bite of the donut and brushed a few green sprinkles off her lap.

"No doubt about that." Grady stood. "I imagine I'll see you at the pub later. You won't want to miss the festivities." He said goodbye and walked toward the gas station.

Sadie would have liked to ask him about Janna's future with O'Paddy's, if he felt it would be a challenge for her, especially while dealing with grief. But she couldn't figure a way to ask without seeming nosy. Well, she *was* nosy. That was her nature. Maybe she'd be able to talk to Janna later. Girl to girl.

Seventeen

Sadie stepped through the back door of the pub, curious to see the preparations for the busy day. She was not surprised to find both bartenders occupied. Janna was wiping down tabletops and setting up plastic holders with drink and food specials. Rafferty was stocking the bar and filling baskets with snacks intended to encourage customers to drink. Music and loud conversation flowed from the kitchen where Sadie knew extra cooks had been brought in to make sure there would be enough corned beef and cabbage in addition to the regular menu items.

"Let's head up to the room, Coco. What do you say?" Sadie waited for the usual yip she received when talking to Coco, but the pup was too occupied looking around, no doubt for Paddy, who wasn't in his usual blanket corner.

"Your dog's looking for Paddy, I bet," Raff called over. "He'll be here later. Janna will run home to get him. A pig has to get his beauty sleep for the big holiday."

Sadie laughed. "I understand. I might just go rest up myself. I have a feeling it'll be a long, hectic day."

"You'd better believe it," Janna said. "The longest."

With that, Sadie headed upstairs and settled into her room.

The idea of enjoying some time in the pub later was appealing, but the thought of spending all afternoon and evening there was too much. It was bound to be crazy, and there was only so much crazy she could take. The whole episode had been nuts from the moment her car broke down to finding out she would have to move into a pub for a few days to the unfortunate demise of the pub owner.

She stretched out on the bed and tried to read but couldn't stop thinking over the events of the past few days. The characters she'd met in Irishton seemed normal, and that made it more difficult to figure out who might be behind Quinn's death. Rafferty and Grady seemed like everyday guys. Drew was... well, a jerk to tell the truth, based on the way he treated Janna. Sadie reminded herself there were often things going on with people that others couldn't see, and that made it hard to size people up sometimes. But there was no excuse for bullying.

Finnian was a bit of an enigma, somewhat outside the circle of interaction between the others. He didn't seem closely connected with anyone in particular, though he appeared to have a casual friendship with Grady. Of course, being new in town, that made sense. It took time to develop relationships with others. The new adult in town was not much different than the new kid in school.

Sadie considered taking someone into her confidence to try to get information and, even better, perspective. But it was hard to know who was trustworthy. Detective Ross, like any other detective, wasn't going to help out. He'd simply want her out of the way while he solved the crime himself. And when she considered talking to others, she reminded herself there was a killer out there. That in itself made it dangerous to pry. Yes, admittedly, prying was exactly what she was considering. If only she could figure out how to do it safely.

Again she tried to read, and this time she dozed off. She awakened to a thundering sound of noise coming from the pub. She opened the door to the hallway and was struck by a combination of bagpipe music, enthusiastic hoots and hollers, and loud bursts of laughter. She could almost picture the scene downstairs, likely the activity she'd observed the past couple of nights but multiplied twenty times or more, based on the way it sounded.

She closed the door again and freshened up, adding a large crystal shamrock brooch to her outfit, something she'd found on a recent trip to Los Angeles to purchase accessories for Flair. She often found favorite items while exploring the downtown streets and meeting with importers. She never knew what she'd bring home, which was part of the fun.

Once she was ready for the evening, she spruced Coco up with a quick hair brushing and clipped a green sequin bow on top of her head. She gathered the pup into her arms and stood in front of a wardrobe mirror.

"We look fabulous, Coco, you see?" She held the pup closer to the mirror, leading Coco into a state of confusion as she appeared surprised to find another dog right in front of her. She yipped at the reflection, which caused Sadie to laugh.

"Don't worry, Coco. I've been known to talk to myself at times too."

The buzz of her cell phone interrupted their mirrored inspection. Sadie set Coco down and answered the incoming call, not surprised to find it was Broussard, likely calling to see if she was staying out of trouble.

"Ms. Kramer."

"Detective Broussard."

It was good to hear his voice, always calm, solid, reassuring. They balanced each other well—her flamboyant personality against his steadfast demeanor. If only they didn't live so far apart, who knew what might develop? For now she was grateful for the friendship and flirtatious attention.

"I called to see if you're staying out of trouble."

No reason to beat around the bush, Sadie thought. She knew he'd been worrying since they first spoke. More specifically, since they first met.

"I'm flattered that you're concerned," Sadie said. "I'm absolutely fine. Coco too. We're about to head down to the pub to see what's going on. It sounds quite lively down there."

Broussard laughed. "I'm sure it does. I don't think you could find a livelier place than an Irish pub on Saint Patrick's Day." His voice became serious. "I want you to be careful though, Sadie. Please. You don't know these people. Remember that first impressions can be deceiving."

"I do understand that."

"Any progress on the investigation?"

Sadie smiled. It was a perfect opening. "I didn't know I was supposed to be investigating."

"Aren't you the funny one? You aren't, of course. I meant the investigation in general. Have they found anything out?"

"Not that I know of. The detective wasn't around earlier, and he's made it clear he isn't going to give me any information."

"Imagine that," Broussard said. "And when you're so willing to help him. What's the matter with these detectives anyway these days? They don't appreciate good help. It's almost like they want to be left alone to solve cases their own way."

"Yes," Sadie said, playing into his game. "I'll just have to make it clear to him that I want to help as much as possible."

"What an excellent idea." Again Broussard laughed. "I'm sure he'll appreciate that."

"I'll make sure he does," Sadie said. "So, Coco and I are dressed up for a night on the town. Which is a night in the pub here since the pub is the heart of the town."

"Then go on out and have a good time. Just be careful."

Sadie could hear the caring in his tone. Even with the light-hearted banter of the phone call, it was clear he wanted her to be safe.

"I will be careful," Sadie said, not wanting him to worry. "I plan to have some of that green beer. I'm daring myself to try it. At least one sip to see if I turn into a four-leaf clover or something like that." She touched the brooch that was clipped on her shoulder.

They ended the call, and Sadie slipped the phone into the side pocket of her tote. Helping Coco into the tote and taking a leash in case it felt safe to let her out, she headed down into the pub.

Eighteen

Whatever Sadie had expected to see once she got downstairs, the scene went beyond anything she could have imagined. Wall-to-wall people filled the pub, most wearing green attire that ranged from plaid jackets to headbands that featured bobbing shamrocks that flashed and lit up. Green beer flowed freely from the bar, with many a gripped mug bearing the traditional beverage. The sea of green swayed back and forth, whether to the live music flowing from a small entertainment stage or as a result of enthusiastic imbibing.

The only spot in the entire room that wasn't packed was Paddy's corner, where he stood in either awe or apprehension, watching the crowd. A barrier fence had been set up to secure his safety. Although all the regulars knew of the pig and were used to looking out for him, this wasn't a normal night, and many had come in from out of town to take part in the festivities.

Raff and Janna were both behind the packed bar counter, filling and serving drinks as fast as possible to crowds of people pressed up against the bar. Grady and Finnian stood against a wall, watching the partying customers together.

With chairs, tables, and barstools all occupied, standing-room-only customers balanced plates of food in their hands, attempting to eat without spilling food or bumping into others. In general, the scene was on the edge of chaos. Yet it was a cheerful chaos, filled with laughter and chatter.

Sadie spotted Detective Ross not far from the pool table, taking in the activity around the room and scanning the crowd in general. When he caught her eye, he made his way over to her, dodging beer mugs along the way.

"Quite a crowd," Sadie said when he arrived.

"Yes, just as expected." The detective looked out into the room, presumably taking advantage of the new spot. "This holiday is always like this. I always hope it stays a notch below a riot. Some years have been better than others."

"Any update on the Quinn Collins case?" Sadie felt the words slip out of her mouth in spite of having promised herself she wouldn't push him for information.

"Nothing I can share," Detective Ross said, just as Sadie expected he would.

"I see all the town regulars are here," Sadie said, hoping it would trigger some commentary.

"So it seems," the detective said.

"Except I don't see Drew," Sadie said. "The guy from that bar up the road." She realized that made sense. Drew had his own bar to attend to. Even though it wasn't an Irish pub like O'Paddy's, it was bound to be busy even if only with customers avoiding the crunch at the pub.

"He may not show up, which would be a good thing," Detective Ross said. "There's usually trouble wherever he goes. Better that he keeps it at his own place. Which reminds me. I should run up there and make sure things are under control."

As the detective headed for the front door, Sadie took another look around the bar, her gaze landing on Paddy's pen in the corner.

"You want to hang out with your friend for a while, Coco?" She directed her question toward her tote bag. If she got a yip or double yip in response, she couldn't hear it over the noise. But she knew the answer.

With her eye on Paddy's corner, she made her way through the crowd, dodging beer mugs and plates of corned beef and cabbage en route. She arrived safely in front of Paddy's enclosure and lowered Coco into the pen. Coco ran immediately to Paddy's side and curled up against him. Paddy grunted, which Sadie took as either a hello or an odd comment of approval.

Deciding she was brave enough to try one of the beverages du jour, she wandered to the bar counter where she managed to find a space between a woman in a green catsuit and a tall man wearing a leprechaun hat. It took a few minutes, but eventually she caught Raff's attention.

"Should I be afraid of that green liquid you're pandering to the crowd?"

"Only if food coloring scares you." Raff laughed. "Otherwise it's just beer. I can make you an Irish coffee if you prefer. Plenty of that going around tonight."

"I'll try the beer," Sadie said, feeling brave. "It'll be a good story to tell if I ever get out of this town."

"Aw, it's not so bad here."

"No, it's really not," Sadie agreed. "Friendly people and a festive atmosphere make an interesting stop along the highway. Don't you think?"

"Sure, usually." Raff stepped away and returned quickly, placing a mug of green beer in front of her. She took a cautious sip and nodded. "It tastes like beer."

"Imagine that." Raff laughed. "And to answer your question, it's not always so friendly in here. Especially in that back room." He glanced toward the door near the pool table.

Sadie asked the obvious question. "Why is that?"

Raff shrugged. "A little money gets thrown around over cards, dice, and table skittles."

"Table skittles?"

"A popular pub game," Raff explained. "A little like bowling but on a table. Sometimes referred to as Devil Amongst the Tailors."

"Are you saying the pub offers gambling?" Sadie asked, partly out of surprise and partly because she didn't mind a good game of poker now and then.

Raff leaned forward and lowered his voice. "I wouldn't call it that specifically."

Sadie took that as a yes.

"I stay out of there unless I need to deliver drinks. Some of the characters who go in and out aren't the nicest people."

"Like that guy who owns the bar up the road?" Sadie knew she was being aggressive with questions, but sometimes it was necessary to get information.

"Drew? Yeah, he's back there often."

"And Ross doesn't get involved?"

"Nope," Raff said. "Honestly, I think Quinn was paying him off to look the other way. It's just amateur stuff, harmless. And every customer helps the business."

"Interesting," Sadie murmured. "But it makes sense."

Raff stepped away to fill more drink orders, and Sadie moved from the bar if only because the crowd of people waiting to buy drinks was becoming claustrophobic. She was often comfortable at large events but not when the crowd was shoulder to shoulder. And this was certainly the case here, quite different from the high-society functions she attended in San Francisco. She even wondered if the occupancy level was higher than it should be. Then again, in a business where a pig was allowed free rein, maybe no one cared.

A number of temporary servers had been hired for the day. They'd come in with the extra cooks, all part of a catering company that was apparently brave enough to tackle the crowd at O'Paddy's. She could only imagine what it was like in the kitchen considering all the food orders flying across the bar counter.

"Can I get you anything from the kitchen?" This question came from a twentysomething girl with green streaks in her shoulder-length brown hair and dangling earrings resembling pots of gold. Her necklace matched the earrings, with a pendant and two clusters of gold coins on either side of that. It was an elegant piece, not one of those dime-store costume items. Sadie wondered if this was something the girl wore every year.

"I could use something," Sadie said, admiring a plate of food held by a passing customer. "But not a whole meal. Maybe something small? An appetizer or snack?"

"I recommend the loaded potato skins," the girl said. Sadie immediately agreed, and the server moved on to take other orders before going to the kitchen.

"Good choice," Grady said, settling in next to Sadie. Both now leaned against the wall. Sadie looked around to see if Finnian had accompanied Grady, but there was no sign of him.

"Any chance you came over to tell me my car is ready?" Sadie was laughing before she even finished the question. She couldn't resist giving Grady a bad time. Not that he deserved it. He'd been very professional in keeping her posted about the status of the repair. But the atmosphere was primed for banter. She couldn't resist a little teasing.

Grady laughed, barely audible over the noise. He shook his head. "Sorry. You're going to have to be patient. Patience, Young Grasshopper. Isn't that the saying? Something like that?"

"Yes, something like that. Though I doubt the original meaning had anything to do with car repairs." Sadie tried to remember where the expression came from. "Is that from the *Karate Kid?*"

"Nope," Grady said. "It's from *Kung Fu,* that David Carradine show."

"Before your time, I would think," Sadie quipped.

"Maybe, but I love those old shows. So many are better than the new ones, where they try to make up for scripting by adding special effects." Grady took a sip of beer while Sadie pondered his statement.

"I prefer the old shows too," Sadie said. "Though more on the mystery side: *Perry Mason, Hart to Hart, Remington Steele,* anything in that realm." Thinking of those made Sadie yearn for a weekend of marathon shows from years ago. Perhaps when she made it back to San Francisco, she would treat herself to one. Then again, if she ever made it to Portland, she was sure to return home with a huge stash of books. She'd need to alternate reading and movie-watching.

And business, of course. This thought reminded her to call Amber at some point to see how the store was doing. Grady excused himself, and Sadie decided to stay put. At least if she remained in the same spot, there was a good chance of the server finding her again to deliver the appetizer.

Sadie took in the activity around the room while waiting for her food order. The pool table had a packed crowd around it, and the dartboard was equally busy. A few couples attempted to dance in front of the small stage area, though the confined space hindered their ability to pull off successful dance moves. Still, they were having fun, and that was what really counted.

The bar continued to be a traffic jam of customers attempting to order drinks. Raff and Janna were moving as fast as they could, both clearly working up a sweat already. Customers gathered in groups around the room, drinking and laughing. Sadie felt sure a few good Irish jokes were being thrown around. And a few bad ones. She doubted it mattered to either the ones telling the jokes or the ones listening.

The server appeared, seemingly out of nowhere, and handed Sadie her order of loaded potato skins. Sadie dug through her tote bag for money and paid the server.

While taking a first bite of the decadent appetizer, she looked around at everyone in O'Paddy's, who were clearly in high spirits. At least almost everyone. Just as Sadie took a second bite, the door to the back room opened and Drew stumbled out, one hand over his nose. He struggled to get through the crowd and out the front door, only making it after shoving a few people aside with his free arm. Detective Ross soon followed him out, and Sadie eased in that direction, hoping to learn what was going on.

Stepping outside into the night, Sadie took a deep breath of the cool air. It was a refreshing, welcome change from the heated room inside. The detective and Drew were just disappearing around the side of the building, so they didn't notice Sadie's presence. Other customers were hanging out in the parking lot, likely trying to get fresh air. She blended in easily with the crowd as she walked to the corner and peeked around it, finding Ross and Drew in an animated discussion.

"Gonna take some time for that to heal," Detective Ross said.

"So what of it?"

"What of it?" Detective Ross sounded impatient. "What of it?" His voice rose. "Why don't you tell me what happened?"

"It was an accident. Don't make a big deal out of it."

"An accident? A fist landed on your nose by accident? I find that hard to believe. I suggest you tell me what was really going on back there."

"Well, *I* suggest you go in and find out for yourself," Drew said.

"Maybe I'll do just that!" Detective Ross shouted.

Much to Sadie's surprise, the detective's tone had become more and more frustrated as the conversation went on. Even more surprising was the fact he trudged around the corner and back into the pub, so occupied with whatever the issue was that he didn't even notice her.

Drew headed for his truck, and Sadie stepped back inside the pub. She took a cautious look around that she hoped appeared nonchalant. Not seeing anything else out of the ordinary, she fetched Coco from Paddy's corner and retreated upstairs to her room. Something was going on, and she was determined to find out what it was.

Nineteen

Sadie leaned back against her pillows, phone in hand. The desire to escape back up to her room was logical. A little break from the commotion downstairs in the pub was welcome, not to mention a chance to think over the heated dispute between Detective Ross and Drew. The impulse to call Broussard wasn't as logical. But when faced with detective questions, what better person was there to call besides a detective? She dialed Broussard's number, and he answered right away.

"I don't understand. Something isn't right," Sadie said, forgetting their usual phone greetings in her haste to talk to him.

"Ms. Kramer."

"Detective Broussard."

"What is it you think is wrong?" Broussard sounded calm though not entirely happy to hear her rambling on about the situation again.

Sadie explained the altercation she'd seen outside. "I don't understand Detective Ross getting so upset with Drew."

Broussard sighed into the phone. "Sadie, detectives are real people, and real people can get upset. We're not immune to feelings even though we try to keep them under wraps when we can."

"That makes sense."

"It's also possible there've been numerous run-ins with this man, which would be frustrating. We like to think we solve problems, so when they occur over and over again, it's discouraging. That could be what's happening with your detective."

"Actually, you're my detective," Sadie said, picking up on Broussard's wording. Immediately she blushed, surprised at the flirtatious comment coming out of her mouth.

Broussard chuckled. "I like the sound of that."

And there she went, her mind suddenly sidetracked onto the connection she felt with Broussard. It had been there since she first met him while on vacation in New Orleans.

"You've made me lose my concentration," Sadie said.

"I think that's a good thing, especially in this case," Broussard said. "Pun intended."

"I suppose so," Sadie admitted. "Maybe I should just ignore what's going on here, keep to myself, and be ready to leave as soon as the car is repaired."

"No maybe about it. Sounds like a wise move."

Agreeing, at least on principal, Sadie ended the call with promises to mind her own business that she might or might not keep, pleased to have heard Broussard's voice, which was always reassuring even if not always in agreement.

"What do you think, Coco?" Sadie lifted Coco up and let her curl up on the bed. She gave the pup the red lobster toy they never traveled without. No matter how many new playthings Coco acquired, the red lobster was her favorite. "We'll just read for the rest of the evening. Maybe take one short trip downstairs to grab another appetizer." A yip indicated the petite canine agreed with the plan. Then again, Coco was a very agreeable Yorkie.

Sadie tried to relax, but her mind kept returning to the scene downstairs. Or make that scenes plural. There was the incident outside the pub between Detective Ross and Drew. But there was plenty going on inside too. To begin with, what was going on in that back room?

A thought began to form in Sadie's mind that was likely to get her in trouble. But that wouldn't stop her from following it. Nothing said the back room was off-limits. There wasn't a sign that she could remember indicating it was for employees only.

Unable to get that thought out of her mind, she helped Coco into the tote bag. Although she planned to let Coco visit with Paddy, the tote bag provided a good backup plan in case the rowdy crowd dictated keeping her closer. After a quick glance in the mirror, she determined she was still presentable enough to head downstairs.

The pub was every bit as festive as it had been earlier, perhaps even more, if that was possible. The music volume was definitely higher, more people danced in front of the stage, and the bar counter was more packed than it had been before.

Paddy was hanging out in the corner pen, nonplussed by the activity. Sadie could almost swear he smiled as she approached and took Coco out of the bag.

"Here you go, Paddy. Your friend is here to visit with you." Coco ran over to Paddy and licked his face, which the pig didn't seem to mind at all. Rather, he wiggled his snout in appreciation.

With Coco settled in, Sadie worked her way through the crowd and stood by the pool table, attempting to look nonchalant. Slowly she moved toward the door, feigning interest in watching the current pool game from a different angle. When it felt least obvious, she slipped through the door into the back room.

If it was possible to step from one world into another instantly, that's what it felt like when she looked around the room she'd just entered. For one thing, no one was there, not a single person. That made no sense. She'd seen numerous people go in and out, and one man had stumbled out after a fight. At least that was what it appeared like. Why would the room be empty now? There were several tables set in such a way that they could be used separately or pushed together for a larger group. Wire holders with condiments rested on some of the tables, ready for diners to sit and enjoy a meal. A couple of tables were clear other than a deck of cards and a wooden game setup of pins with a ball attached by a rope to a pole.

For the most part, the room bore all the marks of a private dining room and none at all of anything sinister. Several things about this made no sense to Sadie. The biggest was the simple fact that the pub was packed with shoulder to shoulder people, many who could be in the back room, helping to keep the main room from being overcrowded. Why would the pub not be taking advantage of all the possible space it had for such a busy occasion?

The other thing that didn't make sense was the occasional comment she'd heard in reference to the room. Detective Ross had specifically questioned Drew about it outside. And he'd gone inside and see for himself what was going on. Yet here Sadie stood, and she could see there was nothing going on at all. Was the room some kind of quick meeting place? A location for fast transactions of some kind? Drugs, perhaps? An exchange of money and goods where it would be less noticeable than in the pub or outside?

That was a solid theory, whether accurate or not. Drug problems plagued towns of any size. It could also explain why someone might want to get rid of Quinn. Had he been threatening to turn someone in? Or involved with transactions himself? Did he owe money that he didn't pay? There were many possibilities.

Sadie continued around the room, arriving at a door that she assumed led outside. Finding it slightly ajar, she peeked through the opening and found an office with computer equipment. She was in the process of analyzing this when a sharp voice jolted her out of her contemplation.

"What are you doing in here?"

Sadie turned to see Finnian in the doorway. He stepped in quickly and closed the door behind him. His eyes looked... Was it angry? Not exactly. Worried? Maybe. Scared? Sadie settled on *surprised* and thought quickly before replying. It didn't seem prudent to say she was snooping around. Instead, she went with another angle, the first one to pop into her head.

"I was looking for Coco." Sadie stepped away from the office door and put on what she hoped was a worried expression.

"I see," Finnian said, although his expression said otherwise. It didn't matter. She'd given a decent reason for being back there.

"But it appears she's not here," Sadie continued, looking under a table for effect. "I'd better check outside. Oh my!" She let both hands fly to her mouth, which she thought a particularly good gesture in light of the supposed circumstance. "All that traffic on the parking lot! I'd better get right out there."

She headed for the door, expecting Finnian to step aside to let her out. Instead he blocked the exit.

"Not so fast."

Sadie exhaled slowly. She'd been sure her ruse was convincing. Apparently it hadn't been. And she had a feeling she was about to find out why.

TWENTY

"Really," Sadie insisted, "I need to get out there and find Coco. I'm worried. She could be running loose. Getting stepped on if inside the pub. Getting into the road if outside. Please let me pass."

"Coco is fine. I just came from the bar area. She and Paddy are having a jolly good time." Finnian's expression seemed to ease at the mention of Paddy and Coco, making Sadie wonder why she was being detained at all. But then he grabbed her shoulders, which sent a shiver of fear up her back. But his expression was only that of concern.

"You need to stay out of this room. Do you understand? There's nothing going on here as you can see."

Sadie looked around, managing to squirm out of Finnian's grasp. He seemed calmer, but she was well aware it could be a cover for something he wanted her to find out. Suddenly it made sense. He was right. She needed to get out of there and stay out. *Is this what had happened to Quinn? Did he discover something he shouldn't have?*

"No problem," Sadie said. "I don't have any reason to have to be back here. It's nice and quiet though, which is appealing. But I have my room upstairs for that if I need to get away from all this activity."

"Good." Finnian stepped aside, and Sadie made a quick escape. She aimed for the bar, debating an order for something stiff to drink. She decided better of it though. Whatever was going on, it would be easier to figure out with a clear head.

She found Coco and Paddy in the corner, just as Finnian had said. And indeed, also as he said, they were having a jolly good time. Coco, much to Sadie's surprise, was riding on Paddy's back, and Paddy was—she was certain she was not imagining it— swaying to a rendition of "Danny Boy," which flowed from the stage. The two were quite a sight, and it didn't take long for Sadie to spot the cause of the unusual behavior. A pitcher of green beer had spilled, the contents running into the enclosure.

Sadie didn't know whether to laugh or cry. The two of them looked adorable in the piggyback stance, enjoying the music and —clearly—the beer. She supposed they would just sleep it off later just like half the customers in the room would be doing. Sadie made a mental note to ask Raff about it when things were calmer. Perhaps he'd seen something to explain why one potbellied pig and one Yorkie were having as much of a good time as the rest of the room.

Sadie picked up the empty pitcher and set it at the end of the bar where used glassware was accumulating. She then settled in against the wall, close enough to keep an eye on the partying animals—the actual animals, not the humans.

Across the pub she spotted Finnian leaving the back room. He stopped to speak to Grady, who was standing by the front door. Then he left. The interaction caused Sadie to wonder if Finnian was up to something and if Grady was involved. She considered reporting the run-in with Finnian to Detective Ross, but upon reflection, thought better of it. Ross was not particularly pleased with her snooping around. And what was she going to report anyway? That she'd gone into the room, found nothing of interest, and that Finnian had told her to stay out? None of that seemed worthy of a police report. She could just imagine the detective's reaction. He'd agree with Finnian that she shouldn't have been exploring in there. There was no point in discussing it with him. In addition, as she ran the encounter over and over in her head, there was really nothing to report. Finnian's stance had been a little strong but not specifically threatening.

She found an empty chair and moved it next to Paddy's pen. The music had changed into a lively *Riverdance* piece, and enthusiastic customers around the room were attempting Irish stepdance, some more convincingly than others. If only she knew how to perform those quick foot movements, she might have gotten up to dance herself. The music was catchy, and she tapped her toes in time with it.

Raff and Janna were still slinging drinks. Both looked exhausted. She wondered if the pub would be open the next day. Certainly they deserved a day off after this much work.

So many questions ran through her mind that it was hard to keep them straight. Finnian, for example, had been kind from the start, offering help when her car broke down. And also when she visited him at the marina, though now that she thought about it, he had looked around while they were talking as if he expected someone else to arrive. Or perhaps he was hoping the opposite: that no one would arrive while Sadie was there. Which led to the inevitable thought that he had something to hide. This also matched his insistence that she stay out of the back room. What did he know that she didn't?

Drew, of course, fortunately absent from the day's events, was definitely *not* a good guy. Hopefully Detective Ross had been successful in discouraging him from coming back around.

Sadie sighed. All things considered, she was no further ahead than she had been the first day. She would just have to try harder.

As the hours moved on, the music got livelier and the crowd grew louder. Raff and Janna were barely making it through the night. Servers and kitchen help took turns filling in behind the bar so they could each take breaks. There was a time long ago—long,

long ago—when Sadie could have hung in there with the best partiers. But those days were over, had been over for decades. She and Coco returned to their room upstairs.

Sadie settled back on the bed again, just as she had earlier, book in hand. But her concentration was no better. The recent events and interactions between locals continued to play out in her mind. She gave up on reading and set her book aside. Instead, she clicked on the small TV and flipped through channels, hoping to find an old show, maybe a *Perry Mason* episode that would take her mind off the mystery at hand. When that didn't work, she tried reading again. Then crossword puzzles. Then another attempt to find something on the television. But it was no use. She just couldn't concentrate. Instead, she lay back on the bed, closed her eyes, and counted leprechauns in sheep's clothing in an effort to fall asleep.

She must have dozed off because when she opened her eyes, the music had died down. She moved to the window, cracked it open slightly, and listened to people bidding each other good night. In a lull between car departures, she heard something that concerned her: the sound of a person crying.

Worried that someone might need help, Sadie checked that Coco was sleeping soundly on her velvet pillow and then proceeded downstairs via the back staircase. Sounds of glasses clinking and pans banging echoed from the kitchen's back door where Sadie figured there was a massive cleanup underway.

She followed the sound of crying to a corner of the back parking lot not far from the kitchen. It didn't take long for her to find the source. Janna sat on a bench, crumpled against the wall, both hands covering her face.

"Janna?" Sadie approached softly, not wanting to disturb her more than she already was. "Are you okay?"

Janna mumbled something in response and lowered her hands. "I'm sorry," she said, recognizing Sadie. "I just couldn't hold it together another minute in there. I've been trying so hard."

"You must be exhausted," Sadie said. "I've been watching you and Raff all day. This is a tremendous amount of work."

Janna nodded. "Yes. It always is on Saint Patrick's Day for obvious reasons. But we had Quinn's help before." At the sound of Quinn's name, Janna burst into tears again. "I'm sorry, Sadie. I just can't believe he's gone!"

"I'm so sorry." Sadie sat down next to her.

"I'd been worried about him," Janna continued. "He was stressed about something, and it was getting worse all the time. He started having panic attacks. He would jump whenever the door opened."

"And he wasn't always like that?"

Janna shook her head. "Not like he was lately. He was always a nervous type, but this went beyond nervous. This was more like paranoid."

"Do you think something was up? Something changed?"

"There must have been something." Janna sniffled and pulled a tissue out of her bartending apron. Several bills floated to the ground, which she picked up and put back in her pocket.

"Was he being threatened by anyone?" Sadie asked.

Janna shrugged. "Not that I know of."

The back door opened, and Raff stuck his head out before Sadie could hear whatever the story was. "Hey, Janna. I could use some help in here."

"Be right there," Janna called back. She stood, fluffed her hair, and straightened her apron. "I'd better go in. It's not right to make him clean up alone. Not with the mess customers left tonight. Hey, thanks for listening."

"Anytime," Sadie said, which struck her immediately as a silly thing to say in view of how soon she'd be leaving. At least she hoped she'd be leaving. Unless Grady was mistaken, her car would be ready soon.

Janna headed back into the pub, and Sadie returned to her room. Coco was still sound asleep, right where she'd left her. It warmed Sadie's heart to see the sweet ball of fur curled up on the velvet pillow.

Sadie poured herself a glass of water and contemplated the discussion with Janna. Of note was the information that Quinn had been more nervous than usual recently. Did Detective Ross know about that? She should have thought to ask Janna. But she had an even better approach: she would ask the detective herself the next time she saw him.

TWENTY-ONE

Grady was easy to find the following morning when Sadie went by the repair shop after a less than healthy breakfast of day-old green sprinkled donuts. At least his legs were. The rest of his body was hidden by a vehicle's hood. The fact that this particular vehicle wasn't her car struck her as either a good or bad sign. It might mean her car was already finished. Or it might mean the part wasn't in yet.

"Good morning!" Sadie was aware she sounded more cheerful than anyone wanted to hear the morning after the night before. But she had slept well after returning to her room, and she was starting the day with that effervescent spirit that people often found annoying at an early hour.

Grady pulled his head out from under the hood and eyed Sadie cautiously. "You are far too cheerful for this early in the day," he said. "I'm still waking up."

Sadie looked at a shop clock on the wall. "It's nearly ten o'clock."

"Yes," Grady said. "Too early. And I don't have the news you're hoping to get. Our parts order came in this morning, and the part your car needs wasn't in it."

"What does that mean?" Sadie wasn't sure how to interpret

this. Did he mean the car wouldn't be ready until some sort of afternoon delivery arrived? Or was he saying she wouldn't be able to pick up her car at all that day?

Grady wiped his hands on a blue rag and tossed it on a workbench under the wall clock. "It means you're going to be visiting our lovely town for another day."

"But..."

Grady held up his hand. "No buts about it. You're here for another day. However, I did talk to the parts people, and they promised it'll be in tomorrow's delivery for sure."

Sadie had mixed feelings about the delay. On the one hand, she still hoped to get to Portland soon. On the other hand, talking to Janna behind the pub the night before had given her insight into Quinn's recent behavior. She could use another day to follow up on that. And she might be able to push Detective Ross for more information. She could also check in with Amber at the shop and contact Broussard to say she was staying out of trouble, which was only a white lie. A super pale white lie. It was not a complete lie, however. She wasn't getting into as much trouble as she *could*. That had to count for something.

"Fine," Sadie said. "I can use the day to figure out what's going on around here."

"Sometimes it's better not to know things," Grady said, ducking under the car's hood again. "What is it they say? Ignorance is bliss?"

"I've never believed in that," Sadie said. "That's the kind of statement made up by people who don't want to get involved."

"Exactly. Smart people." Grady stood and let the hood of the car slam down. Seeing Sadie's worried reaction, he quickly added, "Don't worry, I won't do that to your car. I know a classic when I see one."

"I imagine you do." Sadie was relieved to know he was talking about her car instead of her, though she was the first to admit she was a classic herself.

Sadie nodded and was about to leave when the image of Janna

outside the pub the night before came to mind. "I hope Janna's feeling okay today," she said. "She seems like such a nice person. I hated seeing her so upset last night when the pub was closing up."

"I should check on her," Grady said. "She's taking Quinn's death hard yet still trying to carry on with business." He glanced at the wall clock. "I'll stop by later today."

"I'm sure she was exhausted."

"Definitely. That was one crazy day and night." Grady grabbed a wrench off the worktable and headed toward another car.

Sadie excused herself and left him to his work.

Back at the pub, Sadie arranged to stay another night, looking forward to a quiet evening to follow up the crazy one the night before. She was fairly certain the regular customers had filled their quotas over green beer, Irish coffee, and corned beef and cabbage. It was likely to be an evening of rest for many. And rest sounded good about now.

Sadie stopped by her room to give Coco water and drop a couple of treats in the side pocket of her tote bag, where she liked to keep them handy for times the pup might want one. Which was most of the time, though she did ration them out.

"What do you want to do, Coco?" She waited for the Yorkie's answer, receiving a few meaningful yips in return. "Yes, we could take a walk on the beach if we bundle up." Deciding that was the best suggestion at the moment, she grabbed a purple jacket for herself and a bright red sweater for Coco. This was her favorite of the dozen or so sweaters she had for the petite canine. The red color contrasted beautifully with Coco's golden brown fur.

The beach was cool and clear without a person in sight. With her tote bag over her shoulder but Coco in her arms, Sadie walked toward the marina, which also looked deserted. She figured Finnian was off taking care of other tasks. It was just as well. She wasn't eager to see him after their run-in about the back room.

Seagulls soared overhead, and the ocean lapped against the shoreline with a soft, soothing flow. The contrast between the peacefulness of the beach compared to the insanity of the pub the night before was striking. Sadie could feel herself relax. The fact that her car would take another day to repair set just fine with her. She could have a calm day along the coast to simply enjoy her surroundings.

Sadie approached the marina. There was no sign of Finnian, only a few boats tied to the moorings. Sea kelp had washed up alongside one boat, and Sadie watched it bob in the water as she stepped onto the boardwalk. She strolled to the end of the wooden walkway and looked out at the sea. This was such an unexpected trip in many ways. Somewhere in the craziness of the car repair, the pub atmosphere, and the odd characters around town, she'd found a tiny bit of peace, something she rarely felt in San Francisco, as much as she loved the city. And it wasn't likely to be something she'd find in Portland. Maybe this detour was meant to be.

Sadie let Coco walk around briefly to stretch her legs and then got her settled in the tote bag. When she returned to the pub, she noticed a police car parked out front. Sure enough, Detective Ross was sitting behind the wheel, reading a newspaper. Sadie thought about speaking to him but decided not to, hoping to hang on to the sense of peaceful solitude she'd had on the beach walk. Apparently he had other thoughts. He rolled his window down and called her over.

"Good morning, Detective," Sadie said as she approached his car. "No rest for the weary, I take it? I'd think you could use a day off after yesterday's activity." Coco stuck her head out of the tote and yipped to back Sadie up. Detective Ross frowned at Coco, then brought his gaze back to Sadie.

"I wouldn't mind a day off, to tell the truth, but things keep coming up."

"What kind of things?" Sadie was pleased to see he opened a conversation. Maybe she could find something out. He squashed that thought rapidly.

"I understand you were snooping around the back room in

there yesterday." He nodded toward the pub.

"And how would you know that?" Sadie said, feeling defensive. *Really, how would he know?* "You weren't there."

"I don't need to be somewhere to know what's going on. I have my ways."

Now who sounds defensive? Sadie remained quiet, unwilling to play into his passive-aggressive interrogation. He hadn't directly asked a question, so she wasn't about to volunteer an answer. But she did find it interesting that he knew she'd been in the back room. Did he have "eyes" inside O'Paddy's? Only Finnian had seen her in there, although she supposed anyone could have seen her enter or exit.

Would Finnian have a reason to report her? Maybe to divert suspicion off himself? This, combined with Finnian's attitude when he'd found her in the room, made her wonder for the first time if Finnian had something to do with Quinn's death. That thought caused shivers to run through her. After all, this was the man whose car she'd almost gotten into when her own car broke down. Still, he'd been a perfect gentleman at the time.

Lost in her thoughts, Sadie almost forgot Detective Ross was there, but she snapped back quickly upon hearing his voice.

"Did you hear what I asked?"

"Actually," Sadie said, "I didn't hear you ask me anything, You made a statement about me being in the back room."

"That was a question."

"Technically, it wasn't." Sadie was enjoying the banter by now but knew it shouldn't continue, as much as she loved to cause trouble in situations like this. To play it safe, she used the excuse she'd given Finnian. "I was looking for Coco."

"I already know that's not true."

So much for that.

"Then I was simply looking around. Is that a crime?"

"It's rather borderline. I'd call it a gray area. You were in a place of business, which is private property, and in a room that wasn't part of the event."

Sadie sighed. "That's a stretch, Detective. There *was* a public event going on, and there was nothing posted on that door that said to keep out. So I wouldn't call it a gray area. And that brings up another question."

Now it was the detective's turn to sigh. "And what exactly is that?"

"Why wasn't the room part of the event? The place was packed, and there was plenty of space in there to accommodate people, including tables and chairs where they could sit down to eat instead of balancing plates of corned beef and cabbage in their hands. Do you remember how crowded that main room was? Don't you have occupancy laws around these parts?"

Detective Ross appeared less than amused with her comments, and Sadie decided for once to close her mouth before she aggravated him further. In addition, Coco was getting restless, sticking her head in and out of the tote bag at times and rustling around inside between appearances. Sadie pulled a treat out of a side pocket and dropped it in, hoping to calm her down.

"I'm sorry if I shouldn't have been in there," Sadie said finally, not because she felt an apology was needed but because it would pacify the detective. At least, she hoped it would. "Is there anything else you need from me right now? I feel like I need to lie down. All the excitement is getting to me." She fanned her face with one hand for dramatic effect.

"Nothing more at this time," the detective said. "Just a suggestion that you stay out of places you don't belong. I'm handling the investigation, and I'll solve it without your help."

Well! Sadie bristled. That was just plain rude even though he did have a point. Maybe she *was* interfering by scouting around on her own. Then again, why was he so annoyed? Was she close to finding something out that others didn't want her to know? Obviously, her snooping was problematic for anyone looking to hide something.

Like murder, for instance.

TWENTY-TWO

Janna was behind the bar when Sadie entered. The pub was empty, its regular customers likely sleeping off the holiday. Janna looked tired but somewhat recovered from her meltdown the night before. Sadie decided not to bring it up. If Janna wanted to talk about it, she would.

Paddy was roaming the room, shuffling around, presumably in search of tidbits of food. Sadie received a snort of delight when she lifted Coco out of the tote bag and set her down on the floor. The two trotted and waddled off together as Sadie took a seat at the bar counter.

"Coffee?" Janna held a mug up in the air.

"I could use some, thanks," Sadie said, feeling suddenly weary. The day was catching up to her already, and it had barely begun. "This little detour here is turning out to be anything but relaxing."

"Small town, big drama," Janna said. "It's just how it is with places like this. Especially this one, I suppose. I grew up in a small town, but it was never this extreme. At least I don't remember it being this way. Then again, I was a child."

"Good point," Sadie said. "We see things more clearly when we're adults. Or maybe we don't. We see more but not as clearly."

Sadie stopped, wondering what on earth she was babbling on about. "I really do need that coffee, I think."

"Coming right up. I just made a fresh pot." Janna walked to a coffee maker on the back counter and lifted the pot off the burner. She set a mug down in front of Sadie, filling it with coffee. The enticing aroma wafted up from the cup.

Sadie blew across the surface, took a sip, and sighed. "Perfect. I'll soon be completely awake and everything around me will make sense."

Janna sighed. "Let me know if that works for you, and I'll have some myself. I'd love to have everything make sense."

Sadie nodded. "Better than having it not make sense."

"Now *that* makes sense," Janna quipped, causing Sadie and Janna to smile at the silly banter.

"What makes sense?" Finnian's voice joined in as he took a seat at the counter. Sadie eyed him hesitantly, the conversation outside with Detective Ross coming back to her.

"Everything and nothing," Janna said.

"I'll have what she's having." Finnian tapped his finger on the counter in the direction of Sadie's coffee.

"Holding off on a beer until later?" Janna said as she fetched the coffeepot again and filled a mug for him.

"Yeah, gotta keep a clear head today," Finnian said. "I've got a few things to figure out." He grabbed two packets of sugar from a holder, ripped them open, and poured them into the coffee. Janna handed him a spoon to stir it.

"I know the feeling," Sadie said. "Also, thanks for informing Detective Ross that I was in the other room." She regretted the words as soon as she spoke. When would she learn to keep her mouth zipped?

Finnian stared at her. "What are you talking about?"

"Detective Ross, outside a few minutes ago," Sadie said. "He said he'd heard I was in the back room."

Finnian set his coffee mug down. "I never told him you were back there."

"Oh." Sadie wasn't sure how to respond to that. Finnian could be lying, of course, but what if he wasn't? Who else could have mentioned it to the detective, and more importantly, why would they bother? It didn't make sense.

"You thought I told him," Finnian said. "Why?"

"Because you're the one who came in and told me to get out."

"It wasn't exactly like that," Finnian said in his own defense. "I just didn't want you getting in trouble for poking around where you didn't belong. I'd have no reason to tell the detective you were there."

Sadie considered telling Finnian he'd scared her when he confronted her in the room, but she decided to keep that to herself. "Well, there seem to be a lot of things going on here that there's no reason for, but they're still happening."

"What do you say we just forget the whole thing?"

Sadie searched Finnian's face as if observing a chameleon for the first time. This was hardly the attitude he'd had about it when he first reprimanded her. Were there a couple of personalities at play here? What a strange town she'd fallen into, filled with contradictory people as well. The sooner her car was finished and she could leave, the better off she'd be.

Janna swung by with the coffeepot and topped off both mugs. "I'm not sure what you guys are talking about, but I heard part of it. I know Quinn didn't want anyone hanging out back there. Especially recently."

"That was my understanding," Finnian said. "Anyway, bygones." He lifted his mug toward Sadie as if toasting. Sadie reciprocated the gesture.

"Hey, Finnian," Sadie said, a thought occurring to her. "What's with that second office? The one in the back room? I thought Quinn's office was upstairs."

Finnian's expression changed again. "I thought we were moving on to other subjects."

"That's Drew's office," Janna said. "He rented an empty room from Quinn a few months ago. Quinn wasn't using it for anything, and Drew's bar is too small for an office."

"Another reason to stay out of there," Finnian said. "That extra space is rented to someone else."

"Unfortunately," Janna said, "it just gives him an excuse to hang around." She moved on down the counter to other customers.

"So who would have told Detective Ross I was in that room if it wasn't you?" Sadie switched back to the original subject.

"I have no idea." Finnian took a sip of coffee. Sadie felt certain he was avoiding the question. "There were plenty of people here yesterday."

"Why would anyone care if I went back there at all much less enough to tell the police? No one knows me."

"Maybe that's the problem," Finnian suggested. His cell phone on the counter buzzed with an incoming call, which he glanced at but didn't answer. He finished his coffee quickly, stood, dropped some money on the counter, and left without a word.

"That was sudden," Janna said, walking over to Sadie. "He doesn't usually rush off like that, not without saying goodbye."

"It was pretty abrupt," Sadie said. "He got a phone call that he didn't answer. Maybe he went outside to call the person back and he'll come back in?"

"Maybe. More likely, he'll leave." Janna picked up the money off the counter. "He wouldn't have paid yet if he intended to come right back." Janna walked away to put the money in the cash register.

Strange, Sadie thought to herself. But no stranger than anything else going on around O'Paddy's. She finished her coffee, gathered Coco from Paddy's corner, and headed out.

TWENTY-THREE

Sadie pulled up across the highway from Drew's Place, grateful that Grady had loaned her a car even though the boat of a vehicle wasn't what Sadie was used to. Still, it got her where she wanted to go, which was what mattered.

As she observed the few cars in the bar's parking lot, the black SUV that had looked out of place the other night arrived. It still looked out of place, maybe even more so than before. It pulled into a space between a dusty red pickup truck and a dented sedan of some sort. In comparison, the black car practically sparkled. She recalled Finnian glancing at it with distaste when they'd driven up before. Apparently she wasn't the only one who thought it was a little much for the rural coast.

Sadie turned the engine off and rolled her window down, feeling an ocean breeze that might have been pleasant under different circumstances. As it was, she was too keyed up to enjoy the beachside ambiance. If Drew had something to do with Quinn's death, luxuriating in the ocean breeze could wait. Checking out his place couldn't.

Slipping out of the car, Sadie whispered instructions to Coco, the standard ones for the rare times she left her alone in the car. Do not yip at strangers, stay in the vehicle at all times, limit treats to two maximum—Coco could access the outside treat pocket of the tote bag with some acrobatic maneuvering—and keep the doors locked until Sadie returned. The last wasn't difficult since Coco was too small to reach the automatic door locks with her paws.

Sadie waited for an approaching RV to pass by before crossing the highway, after which she made her way to the side of the building. An Alan Jackson song flowed out through an open window. A few voices blended with the music, creating the dull mixture of sounds one might hear at any bar on a slow day.

The door to the SUV opened, and Sadie put her cell phone to her ear in an attempt to look busy. From the corner of her eye, she tried to identify the driver, but it wasn't anyone she'd met since arriving in Irishton. Something seemed off about both the vehicle and its driver, but it wasn't anything Sadie could put her finger on. Perhaps he was just someone passing through. Yet he'd been there more than one day. She couldn't help but wonder why. A stranger, lingering in a little town. And where was he staying? It was her understanding that the pub offered the only lodging within miles. Maybe he was a friend of a local and was staying with that person. But her instincts told her otherwise.

The man exited the SUV and entered the bar. He walked in an exaggerated manner, like he was playing a part in a movie and the script said to pull into the bar and swagger toward the door, making an entrance, a statement that he'd arrived.

Sadie watched this with interest, still keeping her phone to her ear. If nothing else, doing so would make it unlikely the man would try to speak to her. Not while she was on a phone call. The man didn't seem to notice her, which was exactly what she wanted. He entered the bar, and Sadie decided to follow.

The atmosphere inside was subdued. The music had moved on from Alan Jackson to Garth Brooks, flowing from unimpressive speakers mounted in ceiling corners. Dim lighting offered the kind of setting a person could get lost in if they wanted to, an escape, likely what most customers came to a bar for to begin with.

Drew was nowhere to be seen, which was a relief to Sadie. She'd wanted a chance to observe the place without him.

The man from the black SUV had taken a place at the counter. A female bartender with a shock of red curls pulled back in a ponytail was mixing a drink for him. He looked at his cell phone while waiting.

Sadie took a seat a few places down from him, not close enough to be obvious but within hearing range in case a conversation started up between the man and the bartender. Her timing was perfect because that was exactly what happened when his drink was served.

"You just missed Drew," the bartender said, her ponytail flouncing behind her as she set the glass down.

"Good," the man said. "I don't have anything to say to him." The man glanced in Sadie's direction and quickly looked away.

Sadie ordered a pineapple-and-lime mocktail, having found it refreshing when Raff had fixed it for her. She pulled her cell phone out while waiting for her order, thinking this would make her look occupied. She hoped it would encourage the conversation between the bartender and the man to continue, which it did. The bartender brought her drink and then went back to the conversation.

"I don't feel like talking to him either," the bartender said. "I'm sick of all that attention he pays to Janna."

Sadie took that in, running the interaction she'd witnessed between Drew and Janna through her mind. From what she could tell, Janna had been entirely innocent. Drew had been the aggressor.

The man took a gulp of his drink and set the glass down firmly on the bar counter. "It's a shame what happened to Quinn. I heard he was involved in some shady stuff."

"That's a rumor," Red—obviously nicknamed for her hair—pointed out. "You can't believe everything you hear."

"I guess not," The man gulped the rest of his drink and pushed the glass forward, nodding his head as a request for a refill. Red obliged, quickly making a second drink and setting it in front of him.

The discussion between the two moved on to mundane, everyday topics. Sadie finished her drink quickly, paid her tab, and left a decent tip. *A tip for a tip!* she thought, amusing herself. And she did get a tip out of the short eavesdropping session: the introduction of a new person to the puzzle, one with a jealousy issue.

Returning to her car, she found Coco asleep on the passenger seat and was reminded how absolutely adorable the petite canine was when sleeping. She looked calm and peaceful, nothing like what she'd observed around Irishton. For such a tiny town, it held a huge amount of drama.

Twenty-Four

Janna was working when Sadie arrived back at the pub. That was convenient, as Sadie thought a short conversation was in order. It would involve mentioning her trip to Drew's Place, but it would be worth it in order to get a reaction from the tidbit she planned to casually drop. Red clearly had some animosity toward Janna. It was time to see if that ran both ways.

It was late afternoon by now, and the pub was beginning to fill up as locals came in search of happy hour specials—half-price appetizers and two-for-one well drinks. Those who'd nursed hangovers from the previous evening were ready to start anew. Those who'd avoided the pub on the holiday were now ready to return. It was a jovial crowd yet fortunately calmer than the day before.

Sadie dropped Coco off in Paddy's corner, where the two now greeted each other as if they'd been friends for years. Not only that, but they'd developed quite a fan club among customers who were enchanted with the unlikely pair—one so tiny and furry and one so big and—well—big. Admittedly, they did look adorable together, matching yips and grunts as if speaking some kind of foreign language that only the two of them could understand.

And who was to say that wasn't true? There was much yet undiscovered about how animals communicate with each other.

With Coco and Paddy content, Sadie grabbed a place at the bar and looked over the appetizer menu. In addition to the regular options, a chalkboard behind the bar listed daily specials. Not surprisingly, corned beef was a popular ingredient. Sadie contemplated the corned beef and cabbage soup and corned beef quiche as both sounded enticing. But she stuck with the appetizer menu, choosing an order of Irish potato *boxty*, a type of potato pancake. She came close to ordering Irish soda bread with Guinness cheese dip as well but decided to save room for dinner later. Who knew when she'd have a chance to feast on Irish specialties again.

Janna was in the process of serving a beer to one customer at the end of the counter and something that looked like a strawberry daiquiri to another. When she'd finished, she approached Sadie.

"Still here in Irishton, I see." Janna set a cocktail napkin on the counter in front of Sadie and gave her a sympathetic look. "Grady told me earlier. He feels bad that you're stuck here for another day, if that's any consolation."

"He doesn't need to feel bad about it," Sadie said. "It's not his fault the part hasn't been delivered. I know he's trying. I'll have to let him know I appreciate it."

"I'm sure he knows," Janna said. "You've been very understanding. It must be upsetting to have a trip get messed up like this."

Sadie laughed. "I'd say more intriguing than upsetting. Your town has quite a bit of entertainment value." She stopped, aware that she sounded too lighthearted when the situation in general was serious. "I'm sorry. I didn't mean any disrespect to your uncle. Are there any updates? I haven't seen Detective Ross around."

Janna shook her head. "He hasn't been here today. But I get this weird feeling like he's constantly around. It's sort of creepy."

That took Sadie aback for a moment. If anything, she'd want the detective around in order to find out who the killer was.

"I could go for an order of those miniature potato pancakes," Sadie said, wanting to steer the conversation into a lighter zone. "And a draft please."

"Coming right up." Janna called the food order into the kitchen and then poured Sadie's draft. As she set it down, she looked over Sadie's shoulder. "Well, what do you know? Guess who just walked in. The detective himself."

"Maybe he has some updates on the case," Sadie said. Eager to find out, Sadie turned to watch the detective approach.

"That would be nice," Janna agreed.

But Detective Ross headed toward the dartboard instead of coming to the bar and disappeared into the back room.

The room with nothing interesting in it, Sadie thought. That was clearly not the case. It was just a question of what was so fascinating. And if it had anything to do with Quinn's murder.

The detective emerged a few minutes later and walked to the bar, where he ordered a cup of coffee.

"On duty," he said, pointing to the coffee as Janna poured it.

"Of course," Sadie said. "But when you're off duty, you might want to try their Irish coffee. It's delicious, especially with extra whipped cream on top."

Detective Ross took a sip of coffee after blowing across its surface to cool it. "I just might do that. Thanks for the suggestion."

Janna left in search of additional supplies to restock, and Sadie took advantage of her stepping away to mention Quinn without upsetting her. "I understand from Janna that Quinn seemed especially nervous recently. Do you think that has anything to do with his murder?"

Detective Ross shrugged. "Who knows? Running a business is stressful in itself. Sometimes more than other times. I wouldn't place much importance on that."

"I guess you're right." Sadie decided not to press further. As it was, Janna returned immediately with a jar of green olives and a package of cocktail napkins.

"I'm going to need to order supplies soon. There's so much to do to keep this place going!" Janna's voice cracked, and she wiped a tear away.

"You can do it," Sadie said. "And don't be afraid to ask Raff to help."

Janna nodded. "He's great about that. We've always worked well together." She reached under the counter and grabbed a bus rag.

Sadie turned to the detective. "So any updates?" She figured there was no point in beating around the proverbial bush. He might not want to offer any information, but there was no harm in asking. She waited while he took another sip of coffee.

"Actually, yes," Ross said, surprising both Sadie and Janna, who stopped wiping down the counter to listen.

Oddly, Sadie felt more suspicious than pleased to hear him be so agreeable. If she were a betting person, she'd bet on nothing substantial coming out of his mouth. Still, she waited with a sense of apprehension. Whatever it was, she wanted to hear it.

"We think whoever committed this terrible murder was someone passing through, not anyone local."

"Well, that's a relief," Janna said. It made sense that would be a relief, not just to Janna but to the whole community.

"It's a step forward," Sadie said, realizing the detective was waiting for some kind of response from her. "But how do you know that? Fingerprints?"

Detective Ross shot Sadie a somewhat irritated glance. "You're quite the amateur detective, aren't you?"

"Maybe I am," Sadie said.

"Why does that comment scare me?" Ross took another sip of his coffee.

Sadie understood his reaction. Detectives never seemed pleased when she helped out. They acted like she was interfering. *Imagine that.*

"Just trying to help," she pointed out.

The detective nodded. "Thanks."

Sadie decided to speed the conversation along. "So you found fingerprints that matched someone outside this area?"

Janna delivered the potato pancakes, and Sadie thanked her. She took a bite and sighed. She'd never met a potato she didn't like.

"If you must know, there were no fingerprints at all," Ross said. "But that was a good question. Maybe I should make you a deputy or something like that."

"That would be wonderful," Sadie quipped.

"I was kidding."

"Obviously." Sadie was already getting tired of the pointless discussion. The detective wasn't going to offer up anything substantive. She wondered why she was even bothering to ask him. "But maybe you could give me one of those junior ranger badges or whatever the equivalent is in your department."

"I'll see what I can do."

It occurred to Sadie that Janna had turned away and was wiping down the back counter. Sadie found that odd. For one thing, she'd already wiped that counter down. For another, wouldn't Janna be just as interested in new developments as she was?

"Janna," Sadie said. "What do you think of this?"

Janna responded without turning back toward them. "I guess the killer must have worn gloves or something."

"Very good." Ross applauded, which Sadie thought to be an overly snide response. "Maybe you *both* deserve junior ranger badges."

"We'll be expecting them the next time you stop by," Sadie said. She took a sip of coffee.

Janna turned toward them now, smiling. "I think that's an excellent idea."

Ross finished his coffee and stood up. "Well, ladies, duty calls." He gathered the keys to his patrol car and left.

"Well," Sadie said.

"Well, indeed," Janna said. "That was interesting."

"And entirely uninformative," Sadie said. "Anyone could wipe fingerprints down or wear gloves, local *or* outsider."

Janna nodded. "You have a point there. It makes you wonder why he even stopped by."

"Yes," Sadie agreed. "Yes, it does."

TWENTY-FIVE

Sadie finished her coffee and stood, intending to go up to her room after she fetched Coco. Instead, feeling restless, she decided to take a walk. Janna was already down the counter, taking appetizer orders from two recent arrivals, and other customers were entering. She left sufficient funds to cover her tab and a good tip, gathered Coco—much to Paddy's dismay —and left the pub.

In view of the town's size—or lack thereof—Sadie's destinations for her walk were limited. She could go to the market and see what the bakery shelf had to offer or go to the gas station and harass Grady again about her car repair or go down to the marina. She chose the marina.

A strong breeze hit her as soon as she cleared the buffer of buildings and started across the sand. She glanced up, seeing clouds forming, and suspected rain was approaching. She hadn't thought to check the weather forecast at all since arriving. That was how occupied she'd been with Quinn's murder and her interactions with local characters.

Coco, as usual, would not walk on the sand, so Sadie gathered the ball of fluff into her arms and carried her the rest of the way. She arrived at the marina to find Finnian pacing back and forth.

He stopped suddenly when he saw her standing at the end of the pier.

"Something disturbing you?" Sadie asked before he could offer a greeting. She set Coco down on the wooden walkway.

"Nothing I care to share," Finnian said. "People are more confusing than they seem."

Or perhaps not at all what they seem. "So it appears," she said. "I was just thinking exactly that. Even after only a few days here, I can see something isn't right around here."

That stopped Finnian's next comment, whatever it was going to be. Sadie could see his mind churning, perhaps trying out different responses before choosing one to offer out loud.

"Wouldn't you agree?" Sadie continued. "You're a relative newcomer yourself."

"You're right," Finnian said. "This town is not quite what I thought it would be. To be honest, I suspect I'll be moving on soon." He chuckled.

"Really?" Sadie found that more than a little interesting. Was it possible he wanted to leave before something about him was discovered?

"Anyway, what brings you out here, especially right now?" Finnian looked up at the sky, and Sadie followed his gaze. The clouds had grown darker, and it appeared rain was imminent. Sadie wished she had worn a jacket with a hood, but not only had she not packed one, she didn't even own one. She had a leopard-print jacket back in the room at the pub, which wouldn't have helped even if she'd thought to throw it on.

"I just needed to get out. Detective Ross was hanging around the pub, and he can be irritating."

Finnian smirked. "There's something you and I agree on. What was he going on about this time?"

"Something about fingerprints."

"Really?" Finnian looked surprised. "I wouldn't think he'd give out that kind of information."

Sadie felt a raindrop on her nose and considered making a run for it. "It wasn't really information. He said there weren't any fingerprints to tie the crime to anyone local."

"No fingerprints at all?" Finnian checked the ropes to his boat to make sure it was tied securely. Sadie got the feeling he'd already done this and that it was a way to avoid making eye contact with her.

"None, apparently," Sadie said. "I figure whoever the killer is wiped them clean or wore gloves. I mean, why wouldn't they?"

"Seems like solid reasoning to me," Finnian said. "But I'm not sure it's wise to be offering theories to the detective. It's his job to figure all this out. You don't want to throw him off track. I suggest leaving him alone." His firm tone brought back the memory of him telling her to stay out of the back room.

Sadie shuddered. Another raindrop hit her forearm, and she made a decision to return to town. She picked Coco up again. "I'd better head back."

"Good idea," Finnian said. "Looks like the sky is going to open up any minute. If you go now, you should make it to the pub in time."

Following this advice as well as her better judgment, she made a beeline back to town, but instead of heading to the pub, she ducked into the market as the first blast of heavy rain came down. Seeing Susanna at the counter, she wandered over to say hello.

"New goodies at the bakery counter," Susanna said. "Bear claws and apple fritters. Some chocolate croissants too."

"All sound delicious," Sadie said. "I could use something sweet about now, and I never say no to chocolate."

Susanna nodded. "Tough day? I saw the detective enter the pub. I wish he'd come up with some answers instead of just hanging around."

"I have no idea what his game plan is," Sadie said. "But different detectives work differently. This might just be his style." She thought back to several of the detectives she'd run into over time. Each one did have a certain style about how they worked a case.

"You're probably right." Susanna picked up a loose pen on the counter and put it in a holder with a sign that said Please do not take pens. "I only know Detective Ross. He's been on the local beat for years."

"There aren't any other police in the area?"

"Highway patrol officers pass through, watching for drivers speeding. Sometimes on weekends they hang out to make sure no one leaves the pub who shouldn't be driving. Quinn's always been, er, I mean was, good about that. He'd swipe keys and make people stay upstairs if he thought they needed to sober up before getting behind the wheel."

"Admirable," Sadie said. "And good liability protection for the pub. Businesses can be held responsible if they knowingly let inebriated customers hit the road."

"Good point." The phone rang, and Susanna held up a finger to Sadie while she answered it. "We close at six," she said to the caller before hanging up and returning to the conversation. "We wrap up early here. The advantages of a small-town market. I can't wait to get off work. Janna and I have plans to hang out together."

"That sounds nice, a girls' night." Sadie glanced across to the pub and noted the rain was letting up.

"We'll probably just watch movies at my place. Not much else to do around here, and Janna doesn't like to hang out where she works."

"I'll let you get ready to close up. But I'll take a bear claw to go. And one of those chocolate croissants too."

Susanna rang up the baked goods, and Sadie headed back to the pub.

Twenty-Six

Sadie took the back stairs to her room, braving what was now a drizzle to walk around the building. She'd pop into the pub later for dinner, but she wanted time to relax and mull over the day's revelations, what few there were. She had barely closed the door when she heard voices outside. She moved closer to the window, realizing she'd left it cracked open earlier, not having anticipated the rain. It worked to her advantage, as she was able to hear the voices of two men who sounded not at all happy with each other.

"You're an idiot driving that car down here." The voice was hushed and edgy and sounded a bit like Finnian. In fact, she was certain it was him.

"No one will notice," the other voice said. This one, also male, wasn't one Sadie recognized.

"You'd better hope not," Finnian said, his voice even more hushed. "We don't need the attention. That includes your stupid cowboy swagger. Cut it out."

"Fine."

"And we shouldn't be talking here."

"Agreed."

Footsteps followed, and Sadie waited until the men left before closing the window. Her phone rang as she stepped away. To her delight, the caller ID showed it was her favorite detective, not the one she'd been dealing with locally.

"Detective Broussard."

"Ms. Kramer. I'm calling to see how much trouble you've gotten into since the last time we spoke." His voice was more affectionate than accusatory.

"Very little, I'm afraid," Sadie responded. "I'd hoped to be in more by now. I'll just have to try harder."

"Have they solved the case yet? I haven't seen anything on the police records. But you may be ahead of all that, as much as it pains me to admit it."

Sadie decided to take that as a compliment. Since she was on the scene, so to speak, it made sense that she might know something before it was written up officially. Unfortunately, she didn't, and it wasn't for lack of trying.

"I haven't been able to find out much," Sadie said. "The detective here isn't very accommodating with information. And he's not nearly as charming as you or as entertaining as Froggy."

"Froggy? Oh, yes. The detective in San Francisco who's had the misfortune of your involvement in two of his cases."

"That's not quite fair," Sadie said, although she knew he was teasing. "I was not involved in those cases by choice. I stumbled into them."

Broussard laughed. "A specialty of yours, I believe."

"Perhaps." She had to admit it was true, but she wasn't going to say so directly, at least not to Broussard. "Anyway, there's some kind of issue about fingerprints."

"What issue is that?"

"There aren't any."

Broussard hesitated before speaking. "That's not that unusual," he eventually said. "Criminals usually try to cover their tracks. The prints could have been wiped clean."

"Exactly what I told the detective. Or the killer might have worn gloves."

"I'm sure the detective appreciated your input."

Sadie chose to ignore the affectionate sarcasm. "He feels the guilty party was probably someone passing through, not a local. I disagree. With no prints, it could be anyone."

Again, Broussard hesitated before speaking. "I agree with you, but I hope he's right, that it wasn't a local. I don't like to think of you being close to this person. Speaking of which, is your car still in the shop?"

"Yes, but Grady assured me it would be done tomorrow. It's taken time to get the right part in."

"You might consider getting a newer model Subaru or something like that, at least to drive when you travel."

"That's not a bad idea. I do have two parking spots where I live. And I'm the only driver."

"Coco doesn't drive?"

Sadie wondered how he was even able to say that without laughing. "She's not old enough for a driver's license."

"That's good then," Broussard replied. "I don't condone driving without a license. I would hate to have to give her a ticket."

"She'd probably eat it. She's taken to eating grocery receipts lately if I leave them around. She'd yip that she ate the ticket, her version of 'the dog ate my homework.'"

"This discussion is going downhill quickly."

Sadie laughed. "I agree. So tell me how you are."

"Busy," Broussard said. "Take your little town's situation and multiply it by ten. That's what you'll find on my desk."

"Any without fingerprints?" Sadie didn't know why she asked the question. Apparently the snark gene was acting up in full force.

"I would not be able to tell you, contrary to the apparent behavior of other detectives in the field."

"Or on the coast."

"You're full of quips today."

"I aim to please." Sadie laughed. "But I wish you well in

solving all those cases. It must be stressful." She could almost see Broussard nod through the phone.

"It can be," he said. "I could use a vacation."

Sadie wasn't about to let that pass. It had been too long since she'd seen him. "I hear San Francisco is nice."

"I've heard the same thing," Broussard said. "I was thinking about taking a trip there next month if I can arrange the time off."

"This is the best news I've heard all week."

The vacation to Portland had certainly gone off course. A staycation in San Francisco sounded much more appealing, especially with Broussard involved. They could stroll along Fisherman's Wharf and eat sourdough bread bowls with clam chowder. Then swing by Ghirardelli, whether by accident or accidentally on purpose. Maybe he and Froggy could even meet up for shop talk.

"Any plans for the rest of the day?"

"There's not much in the way of choices here. I'll go downstairs for something to eat in the pub. It'll also let Coco visit with Paddy. They've become close friends."

"An unlikely pair, I must say."

"An interesting pair," Sadie said. "Quite a sight to see. I'll have to remember to take a picture of them together."

"Excellent idea." Broussard answered a desk phone on his end and asked the caller to please hold.

"I'll let you get on with your work," Sadie said.

"Thanks. And try to stay out of trouble, okay?"

"I'll do my best." Sadie ended the call with her fingers crossed. *No point in going to extremes.*

Twenty-Seven

The pub was cranking with energy when Sadie descended in search of an evening meal. Traditional Irish music played over the sound system, and a trio of customers danced in front of the empty stage.

Paddy was in his corner, as usual, with his blankets snuffled into an especially fine bunch. Sadie dropped Coco off to hang out with him and went to the bar to order.

Although she didn't know their names, Sadie was beginning to recognize many of the regular faces. This was a sure sign that it was time to move on, and she hoped, not for the first time, that her car really would be repaired the next day. Spotting Grady at the end of the bar, she moseyed over to double-check the status.

As soon as Grady saw her approaching, he rolled his eyes, which Sadie took as a bad sign. "Don't even ask," he said.

"I hope that's good news, not bad," Sadie said.

"It's good news," Grady said. "The part arrives early tomorrow morning. They're making a special trip out here. You'll have your car by midafternoon."

Sadie nodded. "Great. I need to let the accommodations I had in Portland know that I'll still pick up the last few days of my reservation." She hated to think of the money she'd lost by keeping the booking, but she wasn't about to give up on her destination. Not due to a little detail like a broken-down car in a tiny Irish town where a murder had taken place. However, it did occur to her that she was experiencing something like a plot in the mystery books she liked to read. That in itself was a plus for the trip overall.

"What are you eating?" Sadie said, observing a bowl in front of Grady. "I may need to order some."

Grady called out to Raff. "Hey Raff, can you bring another bowl of Irish stew?"

"Sure thing," Raff called back. "Let me just deliver this pitcher, and then I'll put the order in." He grabbed a full pitcher of beer and took it past the pool table and into the back room. Sadie followed him with her gaze until a voice spoke up.

"Ignore that. It's just for some locals with a game of cards going."

Sadie turned back to see Finnian had joined them. His hair and clothing indicated he'd lingered at the marina during the downpour. He looked at Sadie and then at Grady. "When will her car be ready?"

Sadie sighed, exaggerating it for dramatic effect. "You guys really know how to make a visitor feel welcome, you know?"

"Keep in mind you're the one who's been eager to get your car back," Grady pointed out.

"That's true," Sadie said. "I didn't intend to stay here. But it's been an interesting visit. I'll say that much."

Raff returned to the bar area and called into the pass-through. "Another order of Irish stew! Thanks, Murphy!"

"I recommend a side of Irish soda bread to go with that," Finnian said. "Great for dipping into the juice."

Grady nodded. "He's right about that." Taking a piece of bread from a plate beside his bowl, he dipped it into the stew, took a bite, closed his eyes, and sighed. When he opened them and swallowed, he called over to Raff again. "Add a side order of Irish soda bread, will ya?"

"Got it," Raff replied, spinning back to the pass-through. "And an order of soda bread."

"Any sign of Ross?" Finnian asked, looking around. Without waiting for a response, he excused himself and made the rounds of the room. As he passed the pool table and headed into the back room, the front door of the pub burst open, and an irate-looking Red barreled in, curly red hair loose and flying about. She approached the bar and spoke directly to Raff, who listened to her with a wary expression.

"Where's Janna?" Red's eyes could have shot lightning, that's how upset she appeared to be.

"You know she works days, Red," Raff said. He rinsed out a beer mug and set it aside.

"That doesn't mean she's not here," Red insisted. "I need to speak to her. She needs to stay away from Drew."

Raff picked up two empty glasses off the bar counter where two customers had just left. "Maybe you should take that up with Drew. He ought to be able to control himself and stay away from her."

"You'd think so, wouldn't you?" Red was still steaming. Sadie was immensely glad she wasn't the target of Red's anger.

"I haven't seen her since I took over," Raff said. "She took off right after her shift ended."

"Where did she go?" Red demanded. "You must know."

"I have no idea, Red." Raff was clearly getting irritated. "I'm not her keeper, you know. I'm just another employee."

Red bristled. "You may not be her keeper, but you know more about her comings and goings than anyone else!"

"He said he didn't know." Grady now jumped into the discussion. "And you and Janna go through this over and over, and you always end up friends again. The problem here is Drew, not Janna. It's not going to help coming down here to O'Paddy's and causing a scene."

"A scene? You call this a scene?" Red's face was beginning to match her hair color. Sadie had the fleeting thought that she needed to duck and take cover. And she was right. No sooner had the thought crossed her mind than Red grabbed a tray of olives, cherries, and lemon twists and sent it flying down the bar counter, where it struck a strawberry daiquiri, sending splashes of red in all directions. The realization of what she'd done apparently came over her because she stopped before reaching for a second tray that Raff now held down.

"Are you done with your tantrum?"

Sadie thought for a second that this question came from Raff but soon realized it was from Detective Ross, who had observed the whole episode from the front door. Had they all not been so enthralled with Red's outburst, they would have noticed him enter.

"Yes," Red said, appearing to have run out of steam.

"Then you can come with me." Detective Ross gently took her arm.

"Hey! You can't arrest me for throwing condiments!"

"I'm not arresting you," Ross said. "I'm just removing you."

Red allowed Ross to escort her out peacefully, calling back to Raff over her shoulder, "Thanks for nothing!"

"You're welcome," Raff said to no one in particular. He retrieved Sadie's dinner from the pass-through and set it in front of her.

Sadie took advantage of the food as an excuse to be quiet. She didn't need any verbal interaction at the moment. She just needed to clear her mind, which had only one thought: What the heck just happened?

TWENTY-EIGHT

"Red has always had a thing for Drew," Susanna said when Sadie caught up to her at the market the following morning. "He just never reciprocated it, which makes her angrier than a pig in a greased-pig contest." She lowered her voice. "Don't tell Paddy I said that."

"My lips are sealed," Sadie said as she paid for a chocolate croissant. Day old or not, the one she'd had before was good enough to merit another. If she'd been home in San Francisco, she might have bought a half dozen to keep in the freezer and pull out to have with coffee now and then. As it was, she'd have to settle for one more, which she'd save for breakfast the following morning. Maybe.

"So Red really threw that tray of bar condiments down the counter?" Susanna appeared to mull this over. "Impressive."

Sadie nodded. "I thought so, though the customer with the strawberry daiquiri didn't seem too impressed."

"That's understandable." Susanna stopped to ring up a package of licorice strings for a young boy whose mother helped him with the money transaction.

"It's a crazy love triangle, that's what it is," Susanna said as the boy and his mother walked away.

Sadie quirked an eyebrow. "What is?"

"The whole Red, Drew, and Janna thing," Susanna explained. "Red is after Drew, Drew is after Janna, and Janna is after... No, that's not quite right. It's not a triangle. It's some weird kind of zigzag. Because Janna is not after anyone except Grady."

Sadie leaned forward and lowered her voice. "Drew seems pretty upset about Janna not responding to his advances. Do you think he could have killed Quinn?"

"I doubt it," Susanna said. "Drew is all bark and no bite. I don't think he'd go that far."

"That's what I've observed," Sadie said. "He's a bully, which isn't good, but it's a long way from being a killer. Still, you never know."

Sadie returned to her room above the pub. Picking up her cell phone, she called Flair to check on the shop. Amber answered on the second ring, as she expected.

"How are things?" Sadie settled back against her pillows, Coco curled up by her side. "Busy day yesterday?"

"Actually a good day," Amber said. "You can probably afford a few dozen extra books if you ever make it to Portland."

"Hopefully, that'll be soon," Sadie said.

Sadie exhaled, exhausted at the thought of the ordeal the delay had come to. She'd met some interesting people, gotten a good dose of Irish culture, tried her first green beer, and aggravated yet another detective, a personal specialty of hers. It was a trip she'd remember for a long time, whether she wanted to or not.

"You do find yourself in unusual situations, if I do say so myself." Amber laughed, and Sadie laughed with her.

"I don't deny it," Sadie said. "Broussard has pointed out this very thing to me recently."

"Ah, your handsome New Orleans detective." Amber could never resist teasing Sadie about her fairly recent beau. And Sadie did the same when it came to the growing romance between Amber and the UPS driver, which had taken forever to begin even though the two had danced around each other for ages whenever there was a delivery to the shop.

"He's thinking of coming to San Francisco next month or sometime in the close future. I hope he does. He could use a break."

"And you'd love to see him," Amber said.

"Definitely," Sadie said.

"Once you know, just give me the dates and I'll make sure the shop is covered. Maybe you two can take a drive up the coast."

"Or maybe *down* the coast," Sadie suggested. "The northbound direction doesn't seem to be working out too well for me."

Amber laughed. "Good point. Maybe Carmel or somewhere in that area."

"Big Sur would be nice," Sadie said. "I'll bet he's never been there. It would certainly be a big change from New Orleans."

"You could get a cabin with a fireplace," Amber suggested.

"I'll look into it," Sadie said, imagining the cozy scene.

The shop's front doorbell chimed. "I hear a customer coming in. I'll let you get back to work. Thank you for covering for me, as always!" Sadie said a quick goodbye and ended the call.

It was too early to sleep, too dark to go for a walk, and impossible to go anywhere without transportation. Not that there was anywhere to go other than Drew's Place, and she had no desire to go back there. The thought of curling up with a book sounded inviting, but Sadie was too restless to sit still. For lack of other options, she changed Coco into a favorite leopard-print collar, and they both descended to the pub to see what was going on.

Raff was working the bar alone, as was his normal night schedule. Janna was there, off work, sitting at the counter, cozied up to Grady. Their discussion looked intense, possibly about something serious. Quinn's murder perhaps? Then again, they could be debating what fresh baked goods would show up at the market the next day, a subject that Sadie found personally interesting.

Finnian was finishing up a game of darts to applause from

several around him. When he was done, he took a place at the end of the bar, ordered coffee, and engaged in conversation with Raff, who was between customers. Sadie didn't doubt many considered visits with Raff to be therapy. Bartenders always knew more than they wanted to know about their customers, which explained the times she'd seen Detective Ross approach Raff with questions.

Much to Sadie's surprise, Drew and Red were at the pool table together. Red was taking a shot, displaying fine form, her slender arms holding the cue stick gracefully in a way that told Sadie without a doubt that the willowy woman had studied ballet when she was younger. With her curls loose and free around her shoulders, she was striking.

The only character missing in the mix was Detective Ross, and Sadie had the distinct feeling he'd walk in any minute. Typical of most detectives she'd met, he wouldn't stay away long when he was still investigating the case. And she hoped he would show up, maybe even bearing news.

Sadie sighed. Leaving town without any resolution to the Quinn murder was going to be frustrating. If Ross didn't have any new developments, she'd have to resort to newspapers and the internet to find out how the case resolved. And it was so hard to trust the accuracy of anything online.

As usual, Sadie deposited Coco in Paddy's corner, appreciating the fact that guaranteed dog care had come with her bed-and-beer lodging. Ignoring the fact that the dog sitter was a potbellied pig, it was an ideal situation. Once Coco was settled, she went over to the bar and took a seat next to Janna and Grady. Not wanting to interrupt their discussion, she ordered a beer from Raff and then sat on the stool, facing the room, in order to watch the pub action.

The pub's regulars were beginning to look more and more familiar. An elderly man sitting at a side table raised beets, carrots, and radishes, which he sold at a farmers market twenty miles away. A young lady a few tables away from him worked part-time in the market, filling in for Susanna on her days off. If she recalled correctly, Susanna had said her name was Penny. Or Becky. Or maybe it was Katie. Sadie recognized a few other customers around the room. She had a feeling she'd know every single one if she stayed around a week or so.

It wasn't long before Grady and Janna noticed her, and they both turned on their barstools to face her.

"Good to see you down here again," Janna said. "I understand it's your last night here. At least according to Grady."

"So he says," Sadie answered. "We'll see tomorrow." She looked at Grady and grinned.

Grady held up a hand. "On my honor," he said. "Your car will be waiting for you. I'll even fill the tank, my treat as a thank-you for your patience."

"It was three-quarters full already," Sadie pointed out.

Grady shrugged and grinned. "I never said I was a big spender."

"I have to say I'm surprised to see Drew and Red down here." Sadie nodded toward the pool table.

"Drew's Place is closed one night each week," Janna said. "That's when we see them."

"I guess that makes sense," Sadie said. "There's not anywhere else they can go, is there?"

"Absolutely not a single place." Grady helped himself to a couple of pretzels from a nearby snack bowl and then took a gulp from his draft beer.

Sadie looked at Janna. "It doesn't bother you to see them in here?"

"Not when they're together," Janna replied. "She'll stay stuck to him the whole evening, and he won't bother me with her here. There's trouble when one comes in without the other, but they're okay together. Actually, Red is pretty cool."

"She was in here looking for you earlier," Sadie said. "It was quite a scene."

Janna was nodding even before Sadie finished. "I know. She gets jealous even though she has no reason to be. Drew is the last person I'd be interested in." She sighed. "I admit I didn't help at all by flirting with him back when I made the mistake of dating him."

"You're welcome to flirt with me anytime." Grady slipped his arm around Janna's shoulders and pulled her close to him.

"I just might do that," Janna responded and batted her eyes dramatically.

Grady laughed.

Sadie smiled, glad to see the two relaxed and enjoying time without the bar counter between them. With Janna working the pub's day shift and Grady repairing cars during the day, they had their evenings free, which was a perfect situation.

Watching Janna and Grady reminded her of Broussard's possible visit and Amber's suggestion about them taking a trip together. It was an enticing thought, one she planned to explore. Planning a trip was always fun. The cozy cabin in Big Sur was a particularly appealing possibility.

Detective Ross stopped by and wandered through the pub. He had a few words with Drew and then stepped into the back room. He emerged within minutes, and Sadie seized the opportunity to try one more time to get an update on Quinn's murder. She crossed the room and caught up with the detective by the pool table.

"Excuse me, Detective. I'm going to be leaving town tomorrow, and I was just curious if there were any new developments in the case?" Ross's expression moved quickly from pleased at the declaration she'd be leaving town to annoyed at the inquiry for information.

"If I haven't made it clear, Ms. Kramer, I'm the one in charge of this investigation. Not you, not anyone else, only me. So I suggest you use your last night here to relax and enjoy O'Paddy's."

Sadie contemplated this and then agreed. "Absolutely, Detective. You enjoy your evening as well!"

Returning to the bar area, Sadie took a seat next to Finnian and ordered an Irish coffee. After enjoying a brief conversation, she decided to retire for the evening. She woke Coco up, who was curled next to Paddy. Both had been sound asleep in spite of the bar activity. Paddy continued to sleep, and Sadie was charmed by his adorable snoring as she gathered Coco into her arms and lifted her out of the pen.

Sadie carried Coco upstairs and got the pup settled in her travel palace. She then smiled as she settled into her own bed with only one thought on her mind:

I know who killed Quinn.

Twenty-Nine

A check-in with Grady in the morning confirmed that the part had arrived and Sadie's car would be ready soon. She celebrated with a visit to the Irishton Market for the morning's bakery treat, a pistachio muffin, which she consumed while visiting with Susanna. She would miss their talks after she left. It felt nice to have made a friend during her unexpected stay in the small town. They exchanged emails and promised to stay in touch.

"You know where to find me," Susanna reminded Sadie.

"Yes, I do," Sadie replied. "I just may have to drive up here for the bakery." It wouldn't be the craziest thing she'd done in her life. Impulsiveness was a deeply ingrained trait of hers.

Susanna walked out from behind the counter and hugged Sadie goodbye, wished her well, and made her promise to come back again sometime in the future.

With time to kill, Sadie decided to take one last walk on the beach. She gathered Coco into her arms and headed out. As she started across the sand, she watched the ocean shimmering under the sunlight. She felt a sudden lightness of heart, both from the peaceful scenery and the knowledge she'd be on her way soon.

As she moved along the sand, the idea a killer could be on the loose didn't seem that realistic. Perhaps Detective Ross was right: Quinn had simply been the victim of someone passing through town. An unfortunate, tragic event but not related to the entangled lives of the residents of Irishton in general or the employees and customers of O'Paddy's in particular.

Then again, that brief conversation she'd overheard between Finnian and another man gave her second thoughts. Why would Finnian care what kind of car someone else was driving? What had he meant by not wanting to draw attention?

Sadie thought back to his behavior when he'd confronted her in the back room. Maybe he did have something to hide. Again she felt a shiver run up her spine at the thought that she'd almost gotten into a car with him that first day. And she actually had when he gave her a ride to Drew's Place. It wasn't like her to be so dismissive of safety, so lax about caution.

As Sadie drew close to the marina, she was relieved to see no sign of Finnian. At this point, the less she saw of him before leaving, the better. Really, the less she saw of a few people, the better —Red with her wild temper, Drew with his obvious issues, and Finnian with his confusing behavior. Janna, Raff, and Grady were all delightful. And Susanna had been great, a calm in the Irishton storm.

Taking advantage of the empty dock, she walked down to the end and looked out to sea, again admiring the light on the water. It was a view she wanted to commit to memory, to take with her as she continued her journey up the coast. In a way, despite all the drama, she would miss this town.

She took a mental snapshot of the panoramic scene, including the view looking back to the town, and then started back across the beach. As she reached the main street, she was surprised to see Drew storm out of the pub and drive off. She was even more surprised to see Finnian pull out of the lot in his own car and follow Drew. Both were headed in the direction of Drew's Place.

"What do you think about that?" Sadie said to Coco.

"Talking to yourself?" Raff, headed for the pub with a brown

Irishton Market bag in his arms, stopped in front of the entrance and held the door open for Sadie. "I do that too. I even answer myself sometimes."

"It's the best kind of conversation," Sadie said. "No one argues with you. And you can get any kind of answer you want."

"Valid points," Raff said.

Sadie thanked Raff for opening the door and stepped inside. Raff followed, and they both walked to the bar counter where Janna was filling the condiment tray with green olives and lime wedges. Raff placed the delivery on the counter.

Janna reached into the bag and pulled out a lemon. She breathed a sigh of relief. "Just in time," she said. "Susanna to the rescue. What would we do without her? We almost ran out. I wouldn't want to face a shift without lemons on hand. Thanks, Raff."

"Grady told me you'll be leaving today," Raff said, turning to Sadie. "We're going to miss having you around. And Paddy's going to miss his new friend." He patted Coco's head and offered her a pretzel, which Coco eagerly accepted.

"I think they'll miss each other." Sadie placed Coco in Paddy's pen for one last visit. She was certain that Coco let out a tiny yip of a greeting and that Paddy responded with a soft grunt of affection.

"You should take a picture of them together," Janna suggested.

"Thanks for the reminder!" Sadie pulled her cell phone out and took several. With Paddy in a purple polka-dot bow tie and Coco decked out in her leopard-print collar and matching hair ribbon, they made an adorable pair.

"Hungry?" Janna asked. "I can put an order in for you. Maybe some mozzarella sticks? A cup of clam chowder?"

It sounded tempting, and Sadie felt her stomach growl at the thought. "Let me think about it. I want to run upstairs for a minute to make sure I packed everything." Sadie excused herself and headed up to her room, where her suitcase and Coco's travel palace stood ready to go.

She checked the dresser top and nightstand as well as the bathroom counter and wall plugs. Convinced she wasn't leaving anything behind, she wrote a quick thank-you note on a pub notepad and left it with a tip for housekeeping.

Leaving everything ready to pick up as soon as her car was ready, she returned downstairs to the pub to find Raff now behind the bar. To her surprise, Red and Janna stood off to the side of the room in a huddled conversation. Red appeared to be crying, and Janna was comforting her.

"Is everything okay?" Sadie asked Raff as she sat at the bar.

Raff kept his voice low so that only Sadie could hear him. "Apparently not. Red says Drew has been arrested. I don't know anything more than that."

Sadie glanced at the two women. Red was dabbing her eyes with a cocktail napkin, and Janna was trying to calm her down by rubbing her back. Sadie couldn't imagine what must have happened. Drew didn't seem like the most upstanding guy, but getting arrested put things in a new perspective.

Red and Janna continued to talk for a few minutes before hugging each other and walking away in different directions, Red leaving through the front door and Janna returning to the bar. Sadie gave Janna a sympathetic look but said nothing. Even as outspoken as she tended to be, Sadie knew there were times it was best to remain quiet. This was one of those times. Whatever was going on, she had a feeling it wouldn't be long before things got interesting.

THIRTY

Sadie sat back down and looked over the pub menu. The idea of having something to eat before hitting the road was appealing, and now that Janna was back behind the counter, she was ready to take her up on the offer. She'd grown fond of the pub's loaded potato skins, and this was a chance to have them one more time. She also ordered coffee since she'd be driving, and then she looked around the business that had been home for the past few days.

Since it was early afternoon by now, the room was fairly empty. But a few regulars were present, including the elderly man who raised produce and Susanna's part-time assistant.

Detective Ross entered and took a seat at the end of the counter. He set a newspaper down in front of him and ordered a cup of coffee from Janna.

Sadie had to bite her lip to keep from asking him what had happened with Drew, but she managed. Whatever it was wouldn't take long to come out in a small town. And she was right.

Janna gave Ross a peculiar look. "Why was Drew arrested?"

Detective Ross's expression flickered from confused to surprised to deadpan within seconds before he calmly replied, "I can't talk about it."

Sadie was intrigued by the detective's quick shift in reactions but decided not to address it. *Almost as if he doesn't know.* "Anything interesting in the news?" she asked nonchalantly.

Ross waved the newspaper in the air. "Actually, there is. It seems the investigation here is closed."

"Closed?" Sadie repeated. Janna stopped cutting lemon twists to listen. She and Sadie exchanged glances.

Ross nodded. "It was just as I predicted. Someone passing through. Maybe even a case of mistaken identity or a random killing. Drugs involved or something like that. These things happen."

"I suppose so," Sadie said.

Janna's eyes filled with tears, and Sadie sympathized. The findings Ross was detailing offered no sense of closure, and closure was important to those left behind after tragedy.

Grady entered and sat next to Sadie. He dropped her car keys on the counter. "All done."

"So it seems," Janna said. She sniffled and grabbed a cocktail napkin.

Grady looked confused. "What did I miss?"

"Detective Ross says they've closed the investigation," Janna said.

"That's good, right?" Grady said. "That means they found Quinn's killer." He looked to the detective for confirmation.

"I suspect they have," Sadie mused aloud.

Detective Ross folded the newspaper and stood. He pulled money out of his pocket and dropped a few bills next to his coffee cup. "No, but we're sure it wasn't anyone local."

We'll see about that, Sadie thought.

Grady leaned toward Sadie. "Well, that's a relief."

Detective Ross turned away from the discussion and headed for the door only to be stopped abruptly.

"Not so fast," Finnian said, blocking the exit. He pulled a flat, wallet-shaped item from his pocket, which he opened and held up.

"FBI?" Janna's mouth dropped open.

"I did not see that coming," Sadie whispered to Grady.

"Me neither," Grady whispered back.

"There's only one person who could have killed Quinn." Finnian slid his badge back in his pocket.

"I don't know what you're talking about." Ross huffed. "The case is closed."

"It's about to be," Finnian said. "Sadie, would you like to explain? You're the one who figured this out."

Ross turned to Sadie and glared. "You have nothing to go on. There were no fingerprints."

"Because they were wiped clean by someone who understands crime scenes," Sadie said. "Someone who knew he'd be the one in charge of the investigation and could alter the scene and reports. Someone who could cover up evidence."

"That's ridiculous! The murder weapon was found fifty miles north of here!" Ross looked exasperated. "How do you explain *that*?"

"Easily," Sadie said, recalling Ross's car entering the town from that direction the morning Quinn's body was discovered. "You drove up and placed it there to make it look like the killer was someone from out of town. A clever plan, I must say."

Ross shrugged. "Thank you."

"You're welcome," Sadie said.

"Wait," Ross said, realizing he'd just stuck his foot in his mouth. "*Anyone* could have done that. Anyone *here*, in fact." He spun around to face the room. "And why would I kill Quinn? Why would I risk my career like that? And my life? It doesn't make sense."

"It makes plenty of sense," Janna said, stepping out from behind the bar. "He found out what you were up to, and he was going to expose you as the dirty cop you are. You'd already been forcing him to pay you off to keep quiet about the local gambling."

"Well, that alone wasn't very up-and-up of him," Ross said, as if that negated any wrongdoing on his part. "Bribing an officer is a crime, you know."

"So is taking a bribe as an officer," Finnian pointed out.

"Quinn thought the gambling was just local backroom fun," Janna said. "Not..." She looked at Finnian and swished her hand in the air. "Not all of this hullabaloo."

Sadie wondered who on earth said hullabaloo anymore, but it did seem to fit the situation.

Janna's voice grew louder. "He had no idea this was a gambling... a gambling... whatever it was."

"Syndicate," Finnian filled in. "Wire fraud and money laundering, to be specific." He directed his attention to Ross. "When you found out what Drew was up to, you threatened to expose him if he didn't cut you in."

"Once Quinn found out what was really going on, he was stuck," Sadie said. "He'd lose the pub that he loved if the bigger operation continued, so he was going to turn you in."

"I couldn't let him do that," Ross sputtered.

"That sounds suspiciously like a confession to me," Finnian said. "I think we'll continue this on the way to the office." He reached inside one jacket pocket and then the other, eventually pulling out a pair of handcuffs.

"You could have just borrowed mine," Ross said.

Sadie turned back to the bar counter as Finnian and Ross exited, finding her potato skins waiting. "Want to split these?" she said to Grady. "I'm eager to get on the road now that my car is finally ready and the mystery has been solved."

"O'Paddy's famous potato skins?" Grady rubbed his hands together and smiled. "It's a deal."

THIRTY-ONE

Sadie sat in the waiting room at the gas station, suitcase beside her, Coco in her lap. She'd felt sad saying goodbye to Janna and Raff before leaving the pub. It was nice to know there were good people to carry on Quinn's legacy of a small-town pub. With Janna inheriting the business from her uncle, O'Paddy's would continue to offer a brief respite from the world, and Paddy would be well cared for.

Coco had said her own goodbyes, snuggling up next to Paddy while Sadie gathered her things. It had taken a favorite treat to lure Coco out of Paddy's pen, a sure sign that a true bond had formed between the two.

Now that the time had come to continue on her way to Portland, she felt wistful about leaving. It was a good reminder that sometimes the open road can bring unexpected adventures.

Grady finished the paperwork and invoice, and Sadie met him at the counter. Once she paid her bill, she followed him out front, where her vehicle was waiting.

"I must admit, I've never been so entertained during a car repair," Sadie said as she stood by the Mustang, keys in hand. "It's a rather nice service feature, though perhaps a bit dangerous all in all."

"Hopefully, it's the last time we offer *this* much entertainment," Grady said. "But with a new officer assigned to our area, things should calm down."

"I'm sure it will be less hectic, at least. Not counting Saint Patrick's Day, of course, which I assume will always be a little crazy."

Grady laughed. "We wouldn't want it any other way. We can handle that once a year, just not every day."

"You have a great little town here," Sadie said. "It's a stop I'll remember for years to come, I'm sure."

A new voice chimed in. "I'd be surprised if you didn't."

Sadie turned to see Finnian approaching. He was dressed in khakis and a button-down shirt, quite a change from his marina look. A leather briefcase-type bag hung from his shoulder, and his hair was neatly combed.

"Not hanging out on the boat dock today?" Sadie asked, a twinkle in her eye.

Finnian shook his head. "My work here is done."

Grady grinned. "We're gonna miss you. You're quite an ace at the dartboard."

A black vehicle pulled up, and Sadie recognized it as the SUV she'd seen outside Drew's Place. The driver rolled the window down. "Time to go, Thompson."

"Be right there, Jim."

Sadie raised both eyebrows. "Thompson?"

"Joe Thompson." A grin accompanied the revelation. "Though I really liked the name Finnian Sweeney. It had such a nice ring to it."

"Well, I'll be," Grady said, smiling.

Sadie glanced at the SUV, and the driver waved. She recognized him immediately from Drew's Place. "And I take it Jim is... the wannabe cowboy."

The agent formerly known as Finnian Sweeney nodded. He shook Grady's hand and patted Coco on the head. He then looked at Sadie. "Thanks for not being too much of a pain in the derriere."

"You're welcome. I think," Sadie said, laughing.

The agent jogged to the waiting SUV and got in the passenger side. He waved as it pulled out on the road.

Turning back to Grady, Sadie thanked him for fixing the car as well as for the extra entertainment feature that came with the repair.

"Anytime," Grady said. "Maybe we'll see you here again. Without your car breaking down, of course."

"It would be fun to see how things go with Janna in charge now," Sadie said. "It's a big change, running it on her own, but it sounds like she and Raff did most of the work anyway."

Grady nodded. "They did. And now they'll have a chance to make it more profitable without that payoff going out to Ross." He shook his head. "I can't believe he was blackmailing Quinn all that time."

"Not to mention the much-larger operation going on than anyone knew about," Sadie pointed out.

"Well, one person knew about it," Grady said. "I always knew there was something off about Drew. Who would have ever guessed he'd have connections to Vegas? He set that whole thing up and used Quinn's place to pull it off."

"What a crazy scheme," Sadie said. "I guess from Drew's perspective, setting the operation up in a tiny little town was one way to keep it quiet. And using Quinn's place instead of his own gave him a way to pin it on someone other than himself if the operation was ever discovered."

"Until the feds caught up with him." Grady laughed. "I still can't believe all this was going on right here in Irishton."

Sadie sighed. "What'll Red do now that Drew's Place is closing down?"

Grady smiled. "Now that's a nice surprise. Janna plans to offer her a job."

"No kidding!" Sadie said.

"Yep, it's true. With Drew out of the picture, there's no reason for there to be tension between them. Red will need the work, and Janna and Raff need the help. It's a perfect solution."

"It really is," Sadie said. "I can picture it now."

"You'll have to come back and see it in person," Grady said.

Sadie surprised herself to find she wasn't vetoing the idea. "Who knows? I just might show up next March 17. Coco would love to see Paddy again, and I wouldn't mind more of those loaded potato skins."

"We'll keep an eye out for you then." Grady opened the car door and let Sadie settle in. She rolled the window down.

Grady patted the roof of her car and offered a final wish. "May the road rise up to greet you." He stepped back. "Both of you," he added, including Coco in the traditional Irish blessing.

"Thank you, Grady." Sadie turned the key in the ignition, and the engine fired right up. She smiled, waved, and started up the highway.

"Well!" she exclaimed, glancing quickly at Coco. "That was quite an adventure!" Coco yipped in agreement. "Finally, Portland, here we come."

Passing by Drew's Place, she noted the empty parking lot and CLOSED sign on the door. She was glad Red would now get to be a part of O'Paddy's.

There were many things she'd remember about this roadside delay. The friendship between a tiny Yorkie and a not-so-tiny potbellied pig might be the sweetest memory of all. Aside from the bakery shelf at the Irishton Market, of course.

As she continued driving, Sadie thought ahead to the mystery books she planned to stock up on once they reached their final destination. She was certain she'd find some good ones, but it would be hard to match the mystery she'd just fallen into. Then again, only time would tell.

SHAMROCK SUGAR COOKIES

<u>Ingredients:</u>

Cookies:
- 1 cup unsalted butter, room temperature
- 1 cup granulated sugar
- 1 egg
- 1 teaspoon peppermint extract
- Kelly green gel food coloring
- 3 cups all-purpose flour
- 1-1/2 teaspoons baking powder
- 1/2 teaspoon sea salt

Royal Icing:
- 3 tablespoons meringue powder (I use Wilton brand)
- 1 pound confectioners' sugar
- 5 tablespoons warm water
- Kelly green gel food coloring

Green sprinkles or St. Patrick's Day sprinkles

Instructions:

Cookies:

In the bowl of a stand mixer, cream together the butter and sugar for 2 minutes on medium speed. Add in the egg, peppermint extract, and 1 teaspoon Kelly green gel food coloring. Beat until thoroughly incorporated.

In a separate, medium-size bowl, mix together the flour, baking powder, and salt. Slowly add to the sugar mixture. Mix just until incorporated. If you desire a deeper shade of green, add additional gel food coloring, mixing well to fully incorporate.

Divide the dough in half and wrap each piece tightly in plastic wrap. Refrigerate for at least 2 hours.

When ready to bake, preheat the oven to 350 degrees (F) and line baking sheets with parchment paper.

Sprinkle a flat surface or dough mat with flour and roll out a portion of the dough to about 1/8-inch to 1/4-inch thickness. Using shamrock cookie cutters, cut the dough into shapes and place on the prepared baking sheets.

Refrigerate the shapes for 10 minutes, then place in the oven and bake for 8 to 10 minutes, depending on the thickness. The bottom edges of the cookies should just start to turn golden, although with the green coloring, it's not that noticeable.

Remove cookies from the oven and allow to cool on the baking sheet for 5 minutes. Remove cookies from baking sheet and allow to completely cool on a wire rack.

Royal Icing:

Beat all ingredients until icing forms peaks (7-10 minutes at low speed with a heavy-duty mixer, 10-12 minutes at high speed with a hand-held mixer). Cover icing surface with a damp paper towel to keep from crusting over.

Putting it together:

Tint a portion of the royal icing a light green, if desired. Place the light green icing in a pastry bag fitted with a size 2 or 3 piping tip (or if you don't have, you can always use a Ziplock bag and snip a tiny hole in the corner). Place some of the white royal icing in another pastry bag fitted with a sized 2 or 3 piping tip.

Decorate the shamrocks with the royal icing. If desired garnish with sprinkles.

Or, if you prefer to coat the shamrocks with a thin layer of icing for decorating with sprinkles only, thin a portion of royal icing with water until it is easily spreadable. Spread over the surface of the shamrock cookie and add sprinkles as desired.

Allow the cookies to completely dry then place in an airtight container with wax or parchment paper between the layers. Store at room temperature for up to 5 days.

Royal Icing Tips:

It is imperative that your bowls, spoons, spatulas, beaters and anything else that comes in contact with this icing is grease free. I use Dawn liquid dish soap on these items because I know it will remove any trace of residual grease.

For stiffer icing, use 1 tablespoon less water.

Cover the icing bowl with a damp paper towel or plastic wrap in between working with it.

For longer storage, store in a Ziplock bag in the refrigerator. Icing will keep for one week.

Acknowledgments

Sadie Kramer and Coco have a great time on their fictional adventures, but they only manage to do so with the help of others.

I owe heartfelt thanks to Annie Sarac for polishing up the rough edges of *A Flair for Shamrocks*. Mariah Sinclair deserves a round of applause for the fabulous cover. Elizabeth Christy, Sallie Reynolds, Jay Garner, and Carol Anderson all provided valuable insight into plot development. And Paul Sterrett deserves an award for enduring my daily chatter about the story for months on end.

If you're experiencing a craving for sweets after reading this story, you're in luck. Kim Davis has generously contributed the Shamrock Sugar Cookies recipe at the end of the book. You'll find directions for many more delicious goodies at her blog, *Cinnamon and Sugar and a Little Bit of Murder*.

As always, I'm grateful for the support of amazing family, friends, and readers in my life. Their encouragement is what allows Sadie and Coco to enjoy a world of mystery.

Books by Deborah Garner

The Paige MacKenzie Series

Above the Bridge

When NY reporter Paige MacKenzie arrives in Jackson Hole, it's not long before her instincts tell her there's more than a basic story to be found in the popular, northwestern Wyoming mountain area. A chance encounter with attractive cowboy Jake Norris soon has Paige chasing a legend of buried treasure passed down through generations. Sidestepping a few shady characters who are also searching for the same hidden reward, she will have to decide who is trustworthy and who is not.

The Moonglow Café

The discovery of an old diary inside the wall of the historic hotel soon sends NY reporter Paige MacKenzie into the underworld of art and deception. Each of the town's residents holds a key to untangling more than one long-buried secret, from the hippie chick owner of a new age café to the mute homeless man in the town park. As the worlds of western art and sapphire mining collide, Paige finds herself juggling research, romance, and danger.

Three Silver Doves

The New Mexico resort of Agua Encantada seems a perfect destination for reporter Paige MacKenzie to combine work with well-deserved rest and relaxation. But when suspicious jewelry shows up on another guest, and the town's storyteller goes missing, Paige's R&R is soon redefined as restlessness and risk. Will an unexpected overnight trip to Tierra Roja Casino lead her to the answers she seeks, or are darker secrets lurking along the way?

Hutchins Creek Cache

When a mysterious 1920s coin is discovered behind the Hutchins Creek
Railroad Museum in Colorado, Paige MacKenzie starts digging into
four generations of Hutchins family history, with a little help from the
Denver Mint. As legends of steam engines and coin mintage mingle, will
Paige discover the true origin of the coin, or will she find herself riding
the rails dangerously close to more than one long-hidden town secret?

Crazy Fox Ranch

As Paige MacKenzie returns to Jackson Hole, she has only two things on
her mind: enjoy life with Wyoming's breathtaking Grand Tetons as the
backdrop and spend more time with handsome cowboy Jake Norris as
he prepares to open his guest ranch. But when a stranger's odd behavior
leads her to research Western filming in the area—in particular, the
movie Shane, will it simply lead to a freelance article for the Manhattan
Post, or will it lead to a dangerous, hidden secret?

Sweet Sierra Gulch

Paige MacKenzie isn't convinced there's anything "sweet" about Sweet
Sierra Gulch when she arrives in the small California Gold Rush town.
Still, there's plenty of history as well as anticipated romance with her
favorite cowboy, Jake Norris. But when the owner of the local café goes
missing, Paige is determined to find out why. Will she uncover a
dangerous secret in the town's old mining tunnels, or will curiosity land
her in over her head?

The Sadie Kramer Flair Series

A Flair for Chardonnay

When flamboyant senior sleuth Sadie Kramer learns the owner of her favorite chocolate shop is in trouble, she heads for the California wine country with a tote-bagged Yorkie and a slew of questions. The fourth generation Tremiato Winery promises answers but not before a dead body turns up at the vintners' scheduled Harvest Festival. As Sadie juggles truffles, tips, and turmoil, she'll need to sort the grapes from the wrath in order to find the identity of the killer.

A Flair for Drama

When a former schoolmate invites Sadie Kramer to a theatre production, she jumps at the excuse to visit the Monterey Bay area for a weekend. Plenty of action is expected on stage, but when the show's leading lady turns up dead, Sadie finds herself faced with more than one drama to follow. With both cast members and production crew as potential suspects, will Sadie and her sidekick Yorkie, Coco, be able to solve the case?

A Flair for Beignets

With fabulous music, exquisite cuisine, and rich culture, how could a week in New Orleans be anything less than fantastic for Sadie Kramer and her sidekick Yorkie, Coco? And it is... until a customer at a popular patisserie drops dead face-first in a raspberry-almond tart. A competitive bakery, a newly formed friendship, and even her hotel's luxurious accommodations offer possible suspects. As Sadie sorts through a gumbo of interconnected characters, will she discover who the killer is, or will the killer discover her first?

A Flair for Truffles

Sadie Kramer's friendly offer to deliver three boxes of gourmet
Valentine's Day truffles for her neighbor's chocolate shop backfires
when she arrives to find the intended recipient deceased. Even more
intriguing is the fact that the elegant heart-shaped gifts were ordered by
three different men. With the help of one detective and the hindrance of
another, Sadie will search San Francisco for clues. But will she find out
"whodunit" before the killer finds a way to stop her?

A Flair for Flip-Flops

When the body of a heartthrob celebrity washes up on the beach
outside Sadie Kramer's luxury hotel suite, her fun in the sun soon turns
into sleuthing with the stars. The resort's wine and appetizer gatherings,
suspicious guest behavior, and casual strolls along the beach boardwalk
may provide clues, but will they be enough to discover who the killer is,
or will mystery and mayhem leave a Hollywood scandal unsolved?

A Flair for Goblins

When Sadie Kramer agrees to help decorate for San Francisco's high-
society Halloween shindig, she expects to find whimsical ghosts,
skeletons, and jack- o-lanterns when she shows up at the Wainwright
Mansion—not a body. With two detectives, a paranormal investigator
turned television star, and a cauldron full of family members cackling
around her, Sadie and her sidekick Yorkie are determined to find out
who the killer is. Will an old superstition help lead to the truth? Or will
this simply become one more tale in the mansion's haunted history?

A Flair for Shamrocks

When flamboyant senior sleuth Sadie Kramer's car breaks down outside
a small beach town, the repair lands her in unexpected lodging above an
Irish pub for St. Patrick's Day. With pub games, green beer, and a
potbellied pig named Paddy in the mix, it's bound to be a unique
holiday. An assortment of local characters could be guilty, but only one
is the killer. Sadie and her sidekick Yorkie will need the luck of the Irish
to solve the mystery.

<h1 style="text-align:center">The Moonglow Christmas Series</h1>

Mistletoe at Moonglow

The small town of Timberton, Montana, hasn't been the same since resident chef and artist, Mist, arrived, bringing a unique new age flavor to the old western town. When guests check in for the holidays, they bring along worries, fears, and broken hearts, unaware that Mist has a way of working magic in people's lives. One thing is certain: no matter how cold winter's grip is on each guest, no one leaves Timberton without a warmer heart.

Silver Bells at Moonglow

Christmas brings an eclectic gathering of visitors and locals to the Timberton Hotel each year, guaranteeing an eventful season. Add in a hint of romance, and there's more than snow in the air around the small Montana town. When the last note of Christmas carols has faded away, the soft whisper of silver bells from the front door's wreath will usher guests and townsfolk back into the world with hope for the coming year.

Gingerbread at Moonglow

The Timberton Hotel boasts an ambiance of near- magical proportions during the Christmas season. As the aromas of ginger, cinnamon, nutmeg, and molasses mix with heartfelt camaraderie and sweet romance, holiday guests share reflections on family, friendship, and life. Will decorating the outside of a gingerbread house prove easier than deciding what goes inside?

Nutcracker Sweets at Moonglow

When a nearby theater burns down just before Christmas, cast members of The Nutcracker arrive at the Timberton Hotel with only a sliver of holiday joy. Camaraderie, compassion, and shared inspiration combine to help at least one hidden dream come true. As with every Christmas season, this year's guests will face the New Year with a renewed sense of hope.

Snowfall at Moonglow

As holiday guests arrive at the Timberton Hotel with hopes of a white Christmas, unseasonably warm weather hints at a less-than-wintery wonderland. But whether the snow falls or not, one thing is certain: with resident artist and chef, Mist, around, there's bound to be a little magic. No one ever leaves Timberton without renewed hope for the future.

Yuletide at Moonglow

When a Yuletide festival promises jovial crowds, resident artist and chef, Mist, knows she'll have her hands full. Between the legendary Christmas Eve dinner at the Timberton Hotel and this season's festival events, the unique magic of Christmas in this small Montana town offers joy, peace, and community to guests and townsfolk alike. As always, no one will return home without a renewed sense of hope for the future.

Starlight at Moonglow

As the Christmas holiday approaches, a blizzard threatens the peaceful ambiance that the Timberton Hotel usually offers its guests. Even resident artist and chef, Mist, known to work near miracles, has no control over the howling winds and heavy snowfall. But there's always a bit of magic in this small Montana town, and this year's storm may just find it's no match for heartfelt camaraderie, joyful inspiration, and sweet romance.

Joy at Moonglow

Each holiday season is unique in the small Montana town of Timberton. New and returning guests bring their dreams, cares, and worries, and always leave with lighter hearts and renewed hope for the future. But no season has ever been as special as this one. Because, to everyone's delight, wedding bells will be ringing. Thanks to the heartfelt efforts of many and no shortage of sweet romance, this year will be the most joyful of all.

Additional Titles

Cranberry Bluff

Molly Elliott's quiet life is disrupted when routine errands land her in the middle of a bank robbery. Accused and cleared of the crime, she flees both media attention and mysterious, threatening notes to run a bed-and-breakfast on the Northern California coast. Her new beginning is peaceful until five guests show up at the inn, each with a hidden agenda. As true motives become apparent, will Molly's past come back to haunt her, or will she finally be able to leave it behind?

Sweet Treats: Recipes from the Moonglow Christmas Series

Delicious recipes, including Glazed Cinnamon Nuts, Cherry Pecan Holiday Cookies, Chocolate Peppermint Bark, Cranberry Drop Cookies, White Christmas Fudge, Molasses Sugar Cookies, Lemon Crinkles, Spiced Apple Cookies, Swedish Coconut Cookies, Double-Chocolate Walnut Brownies, Blueberry Oatmeal Cookies, Cocoa Kisses, Angel Crisp Cookies, Gingerbread Eggnog Trifle, Dutch Sour Cream Cookies, and more!

For more information on Deborah Garner's books:

Facebook:
    https://www.facebook.com/deborahgarnerauthor

Twitter:
    https://twitter.com/PaigeandJake

Website:
    http://deborahgarner.com

Mailing List:
    http://bit.ly/deborahgarner